Żanna Słoniowska

THE HOUSE WITH THE STAINED-GLASS WINDOW

Translated from the Polish by
Antonia Lloyd-Jones

First published in the Polish language as *Dom z witrażem* by
Wydawnictwo Znak, Kraków in 2015
First published in Great Britain in 2017 by

MacLehose Press
An imprint of Quercus Publishing Ltd
Carmelite House
50 Victoria Embankment
London EC4Y 0DZ

An Hachette UK company

A CIP catalogue record for this book is available from the British Library.

ISBN (TPB) 978 0 85705 713 6
ISBN (Ebook) 978 0 85705 715 0

Translator's note

One of the characters in this novel is a city, the place that we now call Lviv, in western Ukraine. But over the course of the stormy twentieth century this particular city changed its nationality and name a number of times. Before the First World War it was Lemberg, in Galicia, the northernmost province of the Austro-Hungarian Empire, a territory that Poland had lost in 1772 at the time of its first partition. After the First World War, Galicia was restored to newly independent Poland, and the city was renamed Lwów. When the Second World War broke out in 1939, Polish Lwów was occupied by the Soviets, but then in July 1941, the Germans captured it. In the summer of 1944, the Red Army recaptured it; when the war ended, in 1945, the eastern part of Poland was incorporated into the Soviet republic of Ukraine, and the city became Lvov, the Russian version of its name. Finally, when the Soviet Union collapsed and Ukraine became an independent country, it gained its present, Ukrainian name, Lviv.

Polish literature generally retains the Polish versions of proper names, regardless of historical period, and so in the original text of this novel, Żanna Słoniowska has called the city "Lwów" throughout. That's no challenge for the Polish reader, who is likely to know the history of Lviv, as a former and much-loved Polish city. The story is firmly set there, but as it moves between historical periods, I have chosen to use the Polish name, Lwów, when the historical context demands it, the Russian name, Lvov, for the era of Soviet Ukraine, and the Ukrainian name, Lviv, for that of post-Soviet, independent Ukraine.

*

Here are some key dates and basic information to help the reader with some of the historical events mentioned in the novel.

- **1918–19: the Polish–Ukrainian War.** After the dissolution of Austria–Hungary, newly independent Poland fought against the West Ukrainian People's Republic for control of eastern Galicia. There was fierce fighting in Lwów, famously between the Ukrainian Sich Riflemen, and the Polish Defenders of Lwów, who included the teenage soldiers known as the "Eaglets". Legendary heroes to their own sides, they were buried in the city's Yanivksy and Lychakiv cemeteries respectively, places that have retained their patriotic significance (though to the Poles Lychakiv is Łyczaków, and in this book the name also features as the Soviet era, Russian Lychakov).

- **1918–39: the Second Polish Republic.** Lwów was Poland's third largest city, with a mixed population of Poles, Ukrainians and Jews (who made up a quarter of the population). Polish discrimination against the Ukrainians meant the closure of Ukrainian schools and universities that had flourished under the Austro-Hungarian Empire, and Ukrainians were deprived of opportunities to advance their careers.

- **1939–45: the Second World War.**
  - 1939–41: Soviet occupation.
  - 1941 – July 1944: German occupation. With Nazi encouragement, the Ukrainian Insurgent Army (the U.P.A., known as the *banderovtsy* – "Bandera's men", after the Ukrainian nationalist movement leader Stepan Bandera), carried out pogroms against the Poles in Wołyń (Volhynia) and eastern Galicia, the provinces adjacent to Lwów. Meanwhile, in 1941, the city's Jews were massacred by the Nazis.
  - July 1944: Soviets recapture the city.

○ 1945: The city becomes Lvov, in the Ukrainian Soviet Socialist Republic. Poland's borders are shifted west and, as well as Lwów, it loses the city of Wilno (Lithuanian Vilnius), but gains the "Recovered Territories", formerly part of eastern Germany, including the cities of Danzig (Gdańsk) and Breslau (Wrocław). The citizens of Poland's lost eastern territory gradually move west. Poland becomes the Polish People's Republic under a socialist government loyal to Moscow.

• **August 1991: Dissolution of the Soviet Union.** Ukraine becomes an independent country and holds its first presidential election in December. The city that was Soviet Lvov is now Ukrainian Lviv. Soviet era dissident and independence campaigner Viacheslav Chornovil runs for president, but is defeated by former communist head of state Leonid Kravchuk.

• **2004: The Orange Revolution** peaceful protest rejects pro-Russia president Viktor Yanukovych in favour of Viktor Yushchenko, but in 2010 Yanukovych is re-elected.

• **November 2013 – February 2014: Euromaidan protests** in central Kiev against Yanukovych's rejection of an E.U. Association Agreement in favour of closer ties with Russia. The violent civil unrest that takes place in mid-January claims ninety-eight lives. Yanukovych flees the country and is replaced by pro-E.U. president Petro Poroshenko.

ANTONIA LLOYD-JONES
London, 2017

7

"You suspect," Stephen retorted with a sort of half laugh, "that I may be important because I belong to the *faubourg Saint-Patrice* called Ireland for short."

"I would go a step farther," Mr Bloom insinuated.

"But I suspect," Stephen interrupted, "that Ireland must be important because it belongs to me."

JAMES JOYCE, Ulysses

To me, the word "Mama" is not an image, but a sound. It starts in the stomach, moves through the lungs and the larynx to the windpipe, and sticks in the throat. "You are devoid of musical talent," she often said to me, and so I never sing. Yet the voice that is born deep inside me is her voice, a mezzo-soprano. In fact, when I was inside her, I thought that voice belonged to me, but once I was born, I found it was hers alone. This musical separation of ours lasted twelve years, until the day she died. For a long time after there was nothing, no sound, no colour, just a hole right through by the shoulder blade. And when I finally grew up, I realised that now it was she who was inside me. Now she can't see anything. She is just a voice again, a beautiful mezzo-soprano, while I stand in vain before the mirror, opening my mouth and trying to bring it out of me.

Death

On the day of her death, her voice rang out, drowning many other, raucous sounds. Yet death, her death, was not a sound, but a colour. They brought her body home wrapped in a large, blue-and-yellow flag – the flag of a country that did not yet exist on any map of the world. She was tightly shrouded in it, like an Egyptian mummy, though in one spot on the surface a dark, blood-red stain was breaking through. As I stood and stared at that stain, I was struck by the feeling that someone had made a mistake. At school they'd explained to us that every flag is red, because they're all steeped in the blood of heroes. They told us the story of the worker who was shot dead when he came onto the street to fight for his rights with a white flag – when the gendarmes fired their bullets, his blood dyed the fabric red. But since then everything had changed, and now I knew that the colour red more often brought terror than liberation. And yet, as I stood over Mama's body, I couldn't help thinking that red would have been more fitting.

The red flag was solemn and tragic, but the blue-and-yellow one was relaxed and kitschy. It made me think of a hot summer's day, of a rural rest in the fields. Mama said the blue was the sky and the yellow was the corn. There are moments in life when strange, if not highly incongruous, thoughts occur. If Mama had known what I was thinking then, she'd have been horrified. And so, seconds later, when the men who'd brought her home unwound the flag to show us the ragged wound near her shoulder blade, I stopped focusing on the colours and started to think about her skin. Mama used to undress in front of a tall mirror, never making me feel in the least embarrassed, and then she'd stand there naked, examining herself, often singing as she did so. I would sit nearby, visually stroking her white, freckled skin, her small, firm breasts, and her long legs coated in little red hairs. She was my own personal Snow Queen, as well as all the naked Venuses and clothed Madonnas rolled into one from the albums on the bookshelves. Her body spoke of the fact that it was indeed the spirit, and it would have been perfect, if not for a certain flaw. On her back, near her left shoulder blade, there was a satin-white impression the size of a maple leaf – the only bit of her skin that had no freckles, it looked like a crookedly sewn-on patch. I realised it was a defect, but I loved it best of all. I often asked Mama where it came from. "It's the scar from an enemy bullet," she'd say with a laugh. When I was very small, I took this answer seriously, and imagined the enemies of our system chasing her one dark evening, setting dogs on her, Mama hiding in a phone booth, and the bullet coming through the glass and smashing it into a thousand sharp, glittering slivers, hailing down on her body as it slumped torpidly to the ground. But the truth was different: when she was a little girl, a chain of moles had appeared on her back, something like the birthmark Gorbachev had on his forehead, and the doctors had decided to remove them. That was how the satin hollow came to be there.

So when her body was brought home, wrapped in the Ukrainian flag and unveiled before our eyes, my second thought was of that same bit of her skin. A real bullet had hit her right, freckled shoulder blade, and I realised that by doing so it had brought about a certain symmetry between the satin hollow on the left and the gaping hole on the right. Just like my thought about the flag, this particular thought definitely was not appropriate to the situation. So I stood tense and motionless in the main room where, despite the glaring sunlight, every lamp was on, trying to wipe out all these unpalatable associations. This made a totally blank, white space appear in my head – like the freckle-free impression in her skin, but I had no idea if it was in the left or right hemisphere of my brain. It was July 1988, and my mother had been killed in the unequal fight against Soviet totalitarianism.

On the day of her funeral, it felt as though the sound of the military band was going to blow the ornate façades off the houses on our street. The first notes opened many windows, revealing the faces of people who seemed to be expecting an earthquake or similar calamity.

"For me a public holiday means the sound of a brass band," Mama always used to say, on May 1 or November 7, as we pushed our way through the cordons of militiamen standing in the city centre to find our place on the tribune. Those Soviet parades were the only mass gatherings that did not prompt blind fear in me. There were balloons, hand-held flags, and in particular there was undeniable order, decreed from above. Today's crowd was quite another matter. If there had been a biblical deluge, it would have looked like this.

And with no escape either. I stood at a closed first-floor window as the human torrent surged higher and higher. There was an open coffin drifting on it, with Mama lying inside.

Opposite our house was a militia station, and several uniformed officers were crowded onto a rounded balcony at exactly the level of my window. What if one of them raises his gun and aims it at me, I thought. What an idle fantasy! I'd have died instead of Mama without demur, but I was well aware that on the day of reckoning they'd give a dozen like me for one of her. She was great. She wanted to die. She succeeded.

The river of unfamiliar heads was moving, sighing, murmuring. Its every motion was harnessed to the fear jumping inside me. It had the power to swallow me. In the crowd there were pregnant-looking middle-aged women swathed in calf-length overcoats and grey shawls. I knew what they were hiding under their clothing. There were also men dressed in black, with sticks like fishing rods poking from under their arms. I could guess what that meant. And at the same time I had no idea who these people were, or what they could have had to do with Mama. With her mezzo-soprano voice and her collection of all the world's operas on L.P. records, with her fair complexion, her very long, almond-shaped fingernails, and her habit of reading at table. She had never invited them home, nor had they attended her concerts. They had not exchanged greetings in the street, nor had they been for coffee together at the Armianka. They had not worked with her, or brought her those manuscripts that had to be read at night. But now here they were, weeping and wailing as though a branch had been cut from their tree! Yesterday, a strange woman had rung our doorbell to ask what time the farewell to "our Marianna" would start.

Were they guilty of her death?

I adamantly refused to take part in the funeral. I stood by the window until the last young fellow with a fishing rod had disappeared around the corner of a building resembling an ocean liner, the noise of trumpets had dissolved in the air, and just a few crushed packets of Orbit cigarettes remained on the cobblestones. I turned away from the window and went to play the piano – nobody but me would have called that cacophony playing. Except for Great-Granma. We spent that day in her room, without exchanging a word. In the breaks between exercises, I could hear her scratching the wall with her yellow, manicured fingers, and the sound of the tree growing in our courtyard.

Aba – my grandmother – came home in the afternoon, with dark red rings around her eyes, in which I detected a newly taken decision to devote her whole life to me from now on. This is what she told me about the funeral.

The wave of people carrying Mama's coffin towards Lychakov cemetery kept growing. By the time its head was half way down Pekarska Street and the student doctors had started to join it from each medical school building in turn, its tail end was still winding its way through Halytska Square. The rumours said that militia units were already in wait near the cemetery, but how could that possibly have influenced the flow of the tsunami? When it came to be roughly parallel with the Anatomical Museum, where for many years the hands of the city's official hangman had slumbered in a jar of formalin, impervious to every change of regime, the band stopped playing Chopin. Nor did they play the usual Soviet marches.

17

What happened was that the trumpeters struck up the forbidden Ukrainian anthem, "The Red Viburnum":

"We'll raise the red viburnum with jubilant refrain,
Rejoicing in the triumph of glorious Ukraine!"

Gradually the trumpets were joined by singing – dramatic and bad. The women produced icons from under their coats and up flew the faces of Saint George and Saint Nicholas, and the Archangel Michael too, pallid from many years of lying in cellars and attics.

"Shame on Marianna's assassins!" someone shouted.

"Shaaaame!" a thousand voices bellowed back.

"Shall we avenge her death?"

"We swear to avenge it!"

As though to confirm these words, the men with fishing rods cautiously began to shake them, revealing the proscribed blue-and-yellow flags attached to them. The cortège kept moving forwards, inexorably approaching the three arches of the main cemetery gateway. On Mechnykov Street, at right angles to Pekarska, the trams had already been suspended, and all along the cemetery wall a chain of militiamen had been deployed, shielded by a row of armoured cars. Heedlessly, the demonstrators kept surging forwards.

The moment the coffin-bearers drew level with the tramlines, the conductor of the band, a small, bald gentleman, swiftly raised his large hands skywards. This sign was interpreted instantly – the people began to croon another banned hymn, "The Glory and Freedom of Ukraine Has Not Yet Died".

The militiamen seemed to have been waiting for this moment too.

Obeying the sign, they began to wrestle the icons from the women's hands and the flags from the men's. In turn, this galvanised the men in black leatherette jackets, holding large Alsatian dogs on leads – they rushed after those who had fled down side streets, hiding their coloured cloths in their coat fronts and discarding their rods on the run. The ones who were caught were packed into vehicles.

Aba could not forget a boy with a banner who, seeking to escape, had battled his way to a phone box, but as there was already someone inside it, he had jumped onto the roof. Feeling safe up there, he set the flagpole between his feet and gaily began to give the militiamen the finger. A man in black barked a sharp command, and seconds later a trained dog was also on the roof of the phone box. But Aba hadn't had a chance to see how this scene ended before the cortège entered the cemetery grounds and, passing the graves of the great Ukrainian opera singer Solomiya Krushelnytska, the Polish writer Maria Konopnicka and the Ukrainian poet Ivan Franko, headed up the hill. With black rings around his eyes today, the independence leader Viacheslav Maximovich Chornovil walked in step with the coffin the entire way. For the first time in his life he seemed not to notice that his people were being hounded by dogs, beaten with truncheons and taken into custody. On he strode, staring straight ahead. He must have been considering the fact that he, not Marianna, had been the intended victim.

Few people actually reached the grave site, apart from those who knew Marianna in person. From here, on a rise, they could see the vandalised Eaglets' Cemetery, the number seven tram loop and the secluded villas on Pohulyanka Street.

"The Ukrainian people can be proud of their daughter Marianna, who sacrificed her life for them," said Chornovil solemnly, and it never crossed anyone's mind to mention that Mama wasn't an ethnic Ukrainian.

"Her killers think they have silenced our song. But even today they could hear for themselves that its sound is growing louder!" Just then, as if in spiteful mockery of his words, militia sirens began to howl from below: the demonstrators were still being driven away. A white crane glided across the pure July firmament. Today, Mama was no longer wrapped in a flag – a piece of cloth steeped in blood was laid over her like a sheet. The gravediggers closed the coffin and carefully began to lower it into the ground. That was when Aba burst into tears. Much later I found out what she had been thinking at that moment – just as a pregnant woman becomes lighter when she finally gives birth, a mother who surrenders her child to the earth starts to weigh less too. Perhaps that was why she managed to descend the steep cemetery paths unaided, down to the point where some large orange vehicles marked "Water" were gushing generous fountains onto the battlefield. Her legs, bent by rheumatoid arthritis into an ugly arc, moved with more energy than usual. They were hurrying back to me.

Something else happened that day too – I had my first period. Despite the expectations, instead of a majestic flow of purple and crimson rain, two meagre, dirty-brown streaks stained my under-wear. The world seemed a different place from the one I had imagined it to be.

Boxes

Much later on I found out that I was not the only deserter from Mama's funeral. And it has nothing to do with bogus friends from the theatre, or with somebody who didn't show up because they were afraid for their life. It concerns a man who was just as ready as I to share every last drop of his own blood with her. It concerns Mykola.

He was with the funeral cortège until it reached half way down Pekarska Street, when he slipped away down a side street that crossed Mayakovsky Street, and then Zelena. He lived on Leo Tolstoy Street. There were old oaks growing the entire length of it, like trusses supporting the vault of an invisible temple; to his mind it was a far more suitable place to mourn Marianna than the crowded procession heading to the cemetery.

For years he had thought of the neglected villa on Tolstoy Street as a human body: the two-room flat on the ground floor that he had known since birth was the abdomen; the studio in the basement, inherited a few years ago from his father, was the area below the belt; and the attic, which long ago had determined the direction of his professional interests, was the head. There was also the first floor, where the neighbours had their flat – he ignored this bit when he thought about the house. Now, he suddenly realised, he would never be able to tell Marianna the story of what had happened in the attic, and it felt as though the sniper's bullet were ripping his head apart instead of her chest.

He unlocked the gate, went down the steps, pushed one, a second and a third door open, switched on the light, and lay down on the sofa, which was covered with an old woollen rug. The untouched surface of the paperboard on the easel, the dark lake of vinyl on the record player, the even darker sea of the battered grand piano, the gull wings of books lying with their spines upwards – everything was the same as usual.

Death is like a basement full of sketches, he thought. When I die, they'll find nothing but sketches in my studio – as though I'd never finished anything. And an old piano, which I played pretty badly.

Loud knocking resounded from the floor above. Someone upstairs was banging on the floor with a heavy object.

"Not now!" he shouted irritably.

But the banging did not cease; it was steady and insistent. He counted to ten and screamed: "Stop it, Mother! I'm not hungry!"

On one wall of the studio hung the photograph of a young woman, with a look in her sparkling eyes that said any moment now she'd ascend to heaven – it was not Marianna.

Struck by a thought, he stood up, went over to the wall, took down the photograph and put it on the table. Then he set a ladder against the bookcase, and from the top shelf he started to fetch down some boxes coated with dark material. Inside them were some photographs, categorised and captioned. He took them out and tossed them on the table, which was soon covered in scraps of faces, full on and in profile, hands and feet – for a while he shuffled the pictures like cards. Soon he had shrouded them in a quivering cobweb of ash from the cigarettes he had smoked.

The photograph of the woman ready for her ascension ended up in the middle. She had just the same dark and sparkling eyes as he did, a touch too widely set apart, and just the same thick, strong hair. Back then, in 1988, Mykola had a crew cut, but as the empire gradually collapsed, it had grown longer and longer, like his mother's long, straight hair, which she liked to comb upwards, shaping it into something resembling a pile of silk.

Around it, like the rays of the sun, he spread out seven pictures of himself from junior school days. In every one, even from the official class albums, he was slightly goggle-eyed, making a face or sticking out his tongue. As he looked at them, he couldn't help thinking that he'd been rather a backward child – in the Soviet Union, kids like that were kept locked up, and the mildly handicapped ones were sent to ordinary schools under the pretence that they weren't at all different from the other children.

He surrounded the childhood portraits with some later photographs of his mother, who in time had dropped the biblical expectations, and had also let herself run to fat. He had a soft spot for one of her portraits, in which she was standing on top of a mountain with her arms spread wide, as though announcing to all the world that she'd received it as a gift, and this gesture was to ratify an act of permanent ownership. In a way it was true – she was from the Carpathian Mountains, and her family home was on this one, a few hundred metres below, the house she had left to go to college in Lvov, where she'd met Mykola's father. At her feet he placed his father's likeness, in complete reversal of the real state of affairs.

His father's long arms and legs barely fitted within the frame, and Mykola had inherited his build. His father's gaze – cheerless even in his youth – looked as though it had the power to blow out the walls and ceiling of the studio. His portrait too Mykola surrounded with photographs of himself as a child playing the fool. Funny faces had been one of the few forms of protest at his disposal against the merciless rules of life that were imposed on him: no going out with his friends, just studying and playing the piano; when his father wasn't home, the law was kept by his browbeaten mother. Years later Mykola had understood that she too lived in a form of captivity: she was suffocating amid the solid houses of an alien city and in long queues at the shops. They only led a different life in the holidays, when the two of them took the suburban train into the Carpathians, to his mother's home village, where they donned rucksacks and climbed the mountain, which Mykola also regarded as his personal property, despite the lack of a photograph to prove it.

This time the knocking sounded nearer – she was downstairs, at his door. He sighed, stubbed out his cigarette and went to open it. There she stood, holding a tray with a bowl of soup and some thick slices of bread. Her faded flowery dress and felt slippers contrasted with her tidy pile of hair – in old age she had grown even rounder, and in her eyes she had cultivated a new, insatiable desire for possession – just one mountain was not enough for her by now.

"They've been setting dogs on the people at Lychakov cemetery and piling them into militia vans," she said in a tearful tone.

Without a word he took the tray and shut the door in her face.

Gradually the collage evolved into a heap – he had tired of arranging the pictures, and had started tossing them out of the boxes in any old order: his set designs, rehearsals with actors, Crimean landscapes and the city's historic buildings. At one point, a set of photographs dropped out featuring a gaunt young man in bell-bottom jeans from the era when he'd stopped asking his father for permission to go outside and spent day after day in Valery Bortiakov's studio at the Polish People's Theatre. There he would sketch, cut the pieces for stained-glass windows, and help to build the sets.

From the ceiling a pair of empty eye sockets gazed calmly down at the chaos on the table; secretly he called his father's plaster death mask "The Eye of Providence".

He thought back to this morning. A fellow had been taking pictures of Marianna lying in her open coffin. It was quite unreal: there before his eyes the woman he loved was becoming her own monument, a stiff sculpture stripped of intimacy, and wrapped in the national flag no less. When he saw this he felt two contradictory desires: to lie down beside her, and to get the hell out of there. He was sure she deserved a monument, but he'd have preferred a different one, not visible to the eye, but composed purely of sounds – not so much a monument in fact as a place where the air vibrated, imbued with arias sung by her that would start over again as soon as they ended, without tiring, without a break, without applause. The idea of this invisible tombstone cheered him up a bit, but then it occurred to him that if she had had to go so soon, she might at least have left her voice behind. If there had been some miraculous way to save it, he'd have become its depositary, he'd have preserved it here, in his studio, because most of all he had tried to touch her voice and to possess it by touching Marianna. His fantasies carried him further still, as he imagined running into her house, seizing the coffin, and wresting that matchless voice from non-existence, hiding it under his coat, dashing home with it, eluding militiamen and patriots on the way, and then shutting himself away with it for ever in the basement: it seemed he was a deviant for whom a mere part of his favourite woman would suffice.

A gust of wind blew in at the window, sweeping some of the photographs to the floor – twisted in a heap, they lay there like unwanted items – this brought back an even sharper image of the body in the open coffin and the photographer trying to record something that was already hard and still. He remembered Marianna's nipples stiffening beneath his hands, and it occurred to him that death is a lover with no inhibitions or mercy.

One more cigarette was smoked down to the filter, one more stub was planted in the ashtray flower bed. Straight after, Mykola gathered all the photographs from the table and the floor, put them into a canvas bag and replaced the empty boxes on the shelf. He counted them: ten boxes, with about a hundred photographs in each. Ten boxes, a thousand pictures, his entire life to date. One more, the eleventh, was left untouched: instead of prints it contained old-fashioned photographic plates – he had found them in the attic long ago, they were part of the personal legend he'd never told to Marianna. Then he picked up the bag, took it out to the yard, tipped its contents into a rusty refuse bin and set it on fire.

The small bonfire of rubbish was a thrill for the women living on the first floor, the neighbours whom Mykola ignored. Up on the balcony, they rested their bosoms on the shabby balustrade and watched him in silent condemnation. He stood with his back to them, facing the bin, as streams of dark smoke rose from it. He was thinking of the fact that he had never taken a single photograph of Marianna.

Doors

Every evening Great-Granma locked the front door according to her own elaborate ritual, as if she believed she could protect us from uninvited guests like the ones who had called at her home in 1937, taking her husband away with them for ever. She never revisited that story, though Aba regularly reminded us of it: "That evening they rang the doorbell. Papa said it was a mistake and he'd be right back, kissed me goodbye, and left with the strangers. I never saw him again."

It had happened in Leningrad, where Aba and Great-Granma were living before the war. It's no surprise that at an early age I developed fears of an unexpected ring at the door.

And so Great-Granma always checked first to make sure the outside door, painted in a dark colour, was securely slammed shut, then she turned the key in the lock twice, hung up a solid metal chain and sealed it with another, white, door which she locked too, but with a different key. This arrangement couldn't be opened from the outside, which used to annoy Mama, who liked to come home late, and either had to wake the entire household, or have Great-Granma stay up for hours, waiting for her return.

Each of us had our own set of keys: the long thin one sang falsetto and opened the dark door; the short one with an unusual rounded end sighed in a bass tone and dealt with the downstairs gate; the flat, modern one fitted the letter box and was plainly incapable of producing any sound at all. Only Great-Granma had a key to the white door, and nobody knew where she kept it during the daytime.

This door caused me dreadful anguish. Double-locked, chained and bolted, it aggravated my sense of insecurity, as though I were inside a besieged fortress, and if only single-locked it scattered seeds of danger, seeming to expose us to the invasion of strangers with the power to destroy our world.

The dark, outer door was lightweight. I was capable of giving it a violent slam to express my daily, quite understandable, emotions – I'd be furious with Aba when she told me to dress up warmer before leaving the house. The dark door had a "Judas trap" in it, a round peephole made of plain glass, covered on the inside with a small piece of threadbare fabric. Great-Granma perceived dangers in it as well: for one thing, as soon as the little curtain was raised, the person on the other side would notice that he was being watched, or would know there was someone at home, and for another, as Great-Granma saw it, he had the chance to attack through the peephole.

"First just make a tiny chink, to be sure if it's a strange man or one of ours," she taught me. "A strange man might shove a metal rod through the glass and you'll end up losing an eye!"

The stranger was always male.

If someone buzzed our intercom, we had to run out onto the balcony and look to see who was at the main front door, and if it was someone unfamiliar, we had to shout: "Who do you want?"

It was an intimidation strategy. The person down in the street didn't immediately realise where the voice was coming from, and in bewilderment, staring like a blind man, would start looking for the questioner. Being a floor higher up gave us an advantage, enabling us to repel the attack by saying: "No such person lives here!"

There were frequent mistakes, which caused Aba and Great-Granma immense distress. Suppose a man came along looking for somebody called Pavel Ivanovich Petrov. Nothing out of the ordinary, but you could hear the tension in their voices at once. They'd spend ages wondering who the stranger might be and what it all portended – nothing good, of course.

We lived right in the city centre, and quite often someone would start banging on our door at night. The bell ringing unexpectedly, when we were already in bed, was as thunderous as the trumpets of angels heralding Judgement Day, and cut off the soft domestic past from the violent present like a knife. It could be *them*, and *they* had absolute power over people, free rein to do anything at all to them – kidnap them, kill or torture them. The servants of darkness were bound to be dressed in black.

The white, night-time door was doleful, imbued with melancholy. It moved heavily on its hinges, gave out a dull noise, and had no peephole, and the long key was difficult to turn in the lock. If I got up in the middle of the night and saw that the white door was shut, I was seized with a sense of despair and claustrophobia. Its uniform surface made me think of the Russian word *glukhoman'*, meaning "the back of beyond": the white door embodied remote, boundless Siberia, long transports of convicts, an endless snowy plain, and the clank of manacles.

As I have said, the dark door was also fitted with a security chain, thanks to which, during the day, a gap appeared that served to venti-late our pitiful, windowless kitchen. The gap was wide enough to let through noises and air, but not people: the perfect illustration of a state of limbo, an unsettling sense of being at the same time here and there. I would seek opportunities to put an end to this uncer-tainty, so I'd open the door wide, ostensibly to give the kitchen a thorough airing, or I'd shut it with the excuse that it was cold. What a delight it was to open or close the door at will, what a sweet illusion of power! Whenever I opened it, the mirror hanging in the hall would reflect the stained-glass window on the stairwell, and instead of boiled carrots the kitchen would start to smell of a forest; and when I closed it again, my childish faith that we were safe at home returned in seconds.

Great-Granma didn't trust the chain. Whenever it was stretched between the door and the outside world, she would say we had to listen out, in case someone came along and tried to chop it in two with wire-cutters.

And indeed, sometimes rapid footsteps were heard on the stairs and a figure would appear on the other side of the door – two supple fingers would slide into the chink, scrabbling every which way in search of the blocked end of the chain, one of them would go tense trying to grab hold of it, while I, instead of reaching out a hand and helping from the inside, would lend support passively; when further grappling ensued as the fingers fought with the metal, I'd be dancing on the spot with emotion, until the problem was solved: the fingers would flick off the metal bonds, the subdued chain would strike against the wood, the door would open wide and in would burst a goddess – airy, noisy, lively Mama.

The door-locking rituals were repeated for years on end without change, but the more the Soviet Union shook in its foundations, the more heart Great-Granma put into them. Although she never said it aloud, I suspect she was no supporter of the Soviet regime, but nor was she a fan of those who wanted it overthrown. Most likely she was one of those people who only perceive the specific nature of the system in which they happen to live when it starts to peep in at the windows of their homes. The one that had appeared in 1937 had marked her for life. So the more the people took to the streets, and the louder they spoke about things that had once been wreathed in silence, the more strenuously she made sure our front door was securely locked at night.

When Mama suddenly changed her language from Russian to Ukrainian, about a year before her death, the rite of locking-up was enriched by a new element. Once she had completed the usual ceremony, Great-Granma propped a wicker basket full of dirty laundry against the door, and from the next day she went on doing it for good. That was also when she started talking more and more about "Bandera's men", as she dubbed any Ukrainian patriots. Whenever we were left alone together, she'd tell me how the train carriage in which she'd been travelling to Lwów in 1944 had been strafed by them and that she feared them very much – almost as much as the Germans. Now she felt the same way: once again they were trying to get at her carriage, and whenever she leaned out of the window she saw her own granddaughter – my Mama – leading them. That girl, to whom she hadn't spoken for years on end. That girl, who had defied her to become a singer, and was now defying her ideas about life by fighting for an independent Ukraine. So the dirty laundry basket became another tier in the barricade that for years they had been erecting between each other.

That was also when Great-Granma adopted the habit of intimidating me through language. She'd be waiting in the hall, her body barring my passage.

"Don't go talking out loud in Russian!" she'd warn. "Before you know it, they'll haul you into a deserted yard and torture you!"

The next time she asked if I knew the Ukrainian patriotic poem, "Testament", by heart.

"They catch women and children, drag them to a quiet spot and order them to recite it from memory. If you get it wrong, they'll rape and torture you."

I wasn't afraid; I simply couldn't imagine being lectured in the street about my knowledge of literature, and I didn't believe that poetry could be combined with violence.

On the evening of that day when Mama's body was brought home wrapped in the blue-and-yellow flag, Great-Granma neglected her ritual of securing the front door – it wasn't even properly slammed shut. This was an expression of capitulation: Great-Granma had tried so hard, yet once again *they* had come and destroyed her world. Mama was laid on the table in the main room, and long candles were lit on either side of her. The melted wax left bright marks on the oak parquet. Much later, I found out that Aba had had to buy off several decision-makers to stop them from doing an autopsy and keeping the body at the mortuary; she had managed it thanks to her connections in the medical world – she had once been an admired doctor.

Even so, she was surprised by the lack of K.G.B. intervention. It might have seemed that now *they* were taking care to erase, falsify or hush up the death of which they were guilty. That shot seemed ludicrous in every regard: not only had it missed its target, but in Lvov it had thundered like a bell, bidding the remains of the undecided to come out onto the streets. Mama could have had no greater wish (though not so Aba, Great-Granma or I). In the first days after the shot was fired everyone talked about the circumstances of her death: about the illegal demonstration around Klumba – the square also known as Lvov's Hyde Park Corner – at which free elections were demanded; and about the sniper lurking on the roof of a nearby house, site of the grand Viennese Café before the war. People reckoned the sniper had been ordered to fire at the dissident, Chornovil, but Marianna had been moving about so energetically on the flatbed lorry that she had shielded him. A pneumatic weapon was used, so nobody had heard a bang, but at the sight of the bloodstain blossoming on the singer's beige dress some of the people had taken to their heels. Chornovil had continued the rally. He was reconciled to death – not in the sense of an inner indifference, but rather an indomitable courage trained into him by many years in the camps. His former fellow prisoners called it "pathological". A doctor had come forward from the crowd, Chornovil had entrusted Marianna to his care, and carried on. Efforts were made to shield him, or even to drag him off the lorry by force. But no further shots were fired – to this day nobody knows why. Either way, on that day Chornovil received the gift of eleven extra years of life from Mama. I'm sure he must have remembered that in 1999, at the moment when his car was hit by a truck on the Boryspil highway.

Others remembered too, but not for long. In the first few days people talked and shouted, rang up and came to see us – it aggravated me so much that I felt hardened by a mixture of fury and helplessness, and for many years, whenever I saw icicles of wax dripping onto the floor, that state came back to me. Contrary to the tradition that called for burial on the third day after death, arrangements were made for the funeral to be held next day, and – miraculously – nobody stood in Aba's way when she tried to get a place in Lychakov cemetery, Lvov's foremost necropolis. In fact, in the 1980s there was no ban on burying the dead there yet, but you had to have a number of special permits, which Aba managed to obtain at lightning speed. True, the demonstration that the funeral became was brutally dispersed; true, *they* had been to see the director of the Opera to badger him with questions about Marianna; true, in the months that followed someone kept removing the thick layer of imitation flowers that coated the grave afresh each day. I was actually pleased about this last intervention – the blanket of plastic daffodils disgusted me, and seemed to separate me even further from Mama. Later on they stopped bothering, and the flowers clung to the gravestone for good. Autumn covered them with a blanket of leaves.

From the first day Aba waited for a summons to *that place*. Later she told me she had imagined just such a visit tens of thousands of times. She had assimilated the idea from early childhood: when she was a child of seven living in Leningrad, they had murdered her father, and when she was almost sixty and living in Lvov, they had killed her daughter. Between the first and the second incident she had never stopped hating *them*, and had more or less openly expressed her hatred too. In 1944, when she had ended up in this city, she had decided to become a one-woman resistance movement – she made leaflets saying that Stalin was a criminal and dropped them through people's letterboxes. I'm still at a loss to know why she was never the victim of repression for this act; I have no explanation other than the special care of a guardian angel. She only paid one visit to *that building* on Dzerzhinsky Street, soon after Stalin's death: she had been hounding *them* with official inquiries about her father's fate. On the way *there*, she had removed the hatred from her face, coated it like a canvas in a new primer, and painted on a different expression – purely to extract any information at all from *them*. There she was received by a major with a cynical smirk. He was holding her father's file, but despite her requests it wasn't put into her hands. Enigmatically he had announced that her father had died *somewhere in the North*. He had also added that from now on she needn't carry the stigma of the daughter of an *enemy of the people* – the victims of Stalin's terror had been rehabilitated. She still knew neither the date nor the place of her father's death. *They* took great care to ensure that people spent years living in the shadow of their as if half-killed relatives.

It was all completely different in Mama's case: her death was sucked into a void, it fell into a crack between eras. This time Aba wasn't summoned anywhere – suddenly *they* had other things on their minds.

After that shot, time went by in a different way – it's hard to describe, because it galloped like mad, while also standing still, or perhaps it just vanished entirely. At the Rijksmuseum in Amsterdam there's a bizarre clock: from behind its opaque glass face the figure of a man looms up, who erases the minute hand, redraws it in its new position, moves away, and then reappears a minute later to repeat the entire ritual. As I wonder how the Dutch clock might have looked in the days that I'm describing, I think the man would have drawn the new hands in without erasing the old ones, and once the face had come to look like a sun with sixty rays, he'd have abandoned his job and gone off to sleep in a corner. Present time had become soft and warm – the stone pillars supporting it were melting like wax. The past was being rewritten – every single day more of the falsehoods supporting the old system were refuted. It felt as though the future, fresh and different, were within arm's reach – as though we were sailing on a ship from whose deck we could see a wonderful island, so clearly that we could distinguish the colours of the flowers growing there. In this new land everything was bound to work out well! And how could it be otherwise, when evil had been conquered, the fetters were broken, and the prison gate was standing open? So there we were, drifting on this body of water between the rocks of two eras, and even I could surrender to elation and ecstasy, because I regarded this new future just as Mama would have done; all her hopes were coming true before our eyes. The "Carnival" was happening outside our windows and on our T.V. screen too: the last Soviet tanks left the territory of Afghanistan, and the Berlin Wall came down – with Mstislav Rostropovich playing the cello accompaniment. The Poles took part in their first free elections. The Romanians killed the dictator Ceaușescu. Lithuania declared its independence. Russian cities began to drop their Soviet names.

So in mid-July 1988 they were firing at Viacheslav Chornovil as an enemy of the regime, but in early September he formed the People's

Movement, which was the first alternative to the one and only, ruling party, and in April 1990 he was chosen as its candidate for President of the Lvov Oblast Council. When he took his official seat in the very building to which he had been summoned in the past for some unpleasant conversations, he was greeted with the traditional bread and salt by lady teachers and a flock of toddlers in embroidered shirts.

Naturally, *they* caught wind of the different pace of time too. The order to shoot at Chornovil was probably issued by some ardent commie, come unstuck from reality, blinded by illusions of his own power. The rest were occupied with more urgent matters: burning the archives, gearing up to escape or change their colours, and devising plans to privatise local companies. Nobody tried to obstruct the television crews that transmitted the echo of Marianna's death first to Moscow, and from there to all corners of the empire. She was the main news – just for a single day. After this day, the Opera treated her as if she had never existed; only a few of her colleagues attended the funeral, her roles were instantly reassigned, and her name was wiped from the posters: so what if the crowd was chanting it in the streets?

I began to rebel. I wrote letters to magazines and to the director of the Opera. At school I organised gatherings to listen to cassettes on which Mama's voice had survived. I mouthed off at the history teacher, a communist, who was freely making scornful remarks about her death. I wore her clothes and tidied her papers; I set up a sort of museum in her bedroom with all her favourite things in their places. This fight to memorialise her life became my obsession, and helped me to get through the first, terrible years without her.

But this too was bound to come to an end one day: the ship sailed on.

The 1990s arrived, and so did cold, hunger, and planned power cuts. I grew up, and everything Ukrainian began to seem backward, ugly and not mine. I had mentally hushed that already muffled shot, and the operatic arias too – I didn't know how to free myself of the question of whether Mama had died for a just cause or not. I moved into her bedroom, and instead of the portrait of Solomiya Krushelnytska, I hung Freddie Mercury and Jesus Christ on the wall.

In the first years after the shot Great-Granma stopped bothering with the ritual door-locking. We would go to bed without extra protection, which brought me a degree of relief: the worst had already happened, so we could take a break from being afraid. After some time it all began again: the dark door, the chain, the light door. Perhaps she did it for my sake. Though in fact she no longer moved the basket into place. The mouldering wicker basket for dirty clothes had so many holes by now that it couldn't be shifted to and fro – it would surely have fallen apart.

Home

Her sheepskin coat was like an animal hide, her hair was well hidden under her headscarf. She had no first name, no surname or address, but from time to time she'd appear in our weakly lit hallway, making wet footprints with her rubber boots. She'd remove the dirty sheet bundled on her back and unwrap it on the table.

"*Svizhenke telyatko, berit, pani!*" she would advertise her wares in Ukrainian.

Inside there was meat: the butchered pieces were dusted in a white snow of fat, with hair and spots of blood.

"The calf was freshly killed this morning, take it, lady, take it!" she went on.

I remember being very surprised when I heard Aba calling her a "young woman". It couldn't be true – she was sexless, ageless, not of this urban world, in which people travelled by tram, bought fancy cakes at the patisserie or walked lapdogs on a lead.

"It's fresh and I'm selling it cheap, lady!"

I would look at the something spread on the sheet that only that morning had been a live animal. I'd imagine her moving towards it with a sharpened hatchet.

"It's fresh, lady!"

Chop, chop – out pours the blood, the calf's legs give way, she hacks it to pieces, wraps it in her bundle and hurries off to catch the suburban train. Nobody stops her on the journey, nobody checks her identity card, though her path is marked by dark-brown liquid.

Aba would doggedly haggle with her: "Bring the price down a bit, madam!"

She would transfer the butchered pieces from the sheet onto a portable kitchen scale, and examine it from all sides without disgust.

I would be thinking about the slaughtered calf's little legs, which would never run again. The visitor had thick woollen stockings on hers – only children wore that sort in the city, yet more proof that she couldn't be a woman.

The price would be agreed, the animal parts divided forever: some small pieces were put into our fridge, while the rest of it was packed into the sheet again. Then it was time for an exchange of niceties.

"How's your husband? The children? Your mother? Is the sowing done? Has the crop come up?"

"*Dobre! Dobre! Dobre!*" – "Fine, fine, fine!" the woman would reply, sighing wistfully, as if she were really saying: "*Pohano! Pohano! Pohano!*" – "Awful, awful, awful!"

She never took off the sheepskin coat, and she never went beyond the range of the dark hallway.

Chop, chop went the hatchet, I'd think, and although she'd be gone by now, I could still hear her voice: "*Telyatko svizhe, horosze, shchoyno syohodni zarubala*" – "Nice fresh little calf, only slaughtered today."

The picture hanging in Great-Granma's room was of a dark face, with streams of blood pouring down it.

"Evil people killed him – they split his hands open with sharp nails."

When? How? What for? I didn't know. I wasn't allowed to listen to Great-Granma or to look at the painting, because it was evil. The creature with the meat wasn't evil.

The curtains in Great-Granma's room were hardly ever opened, and it was rarely ventilated. The unmade bed bristled with dirty yellow sheets, and beside it stood a large enamel chamber pot with a lid. From dawn to dusk Great-Granma went about in her dressing gown and almost never left the house. Like a Christmas tree festooned with garlands, she was draped in bands of wrinkled white skin, pleasant to the touch. The skin on her head was pink and springy, covered in thinning white hair cut in a bob. Distorted by the thick glass in her spectacles, her eyes were like two suckerfish, stuck to the aquarium wall.

I would go in there to play the piano, but first I had to listen to her talking about God in the picture: he had a green face, long hair, and a wreath made of twigs on his head.

"It hurt the darling Jesus very, very much when those evil people jabbed holes in his hands. The blood spurted in all directions. But they went on banging in the nails with a hammer."

Great-Granma would gently pin me to the wall, while I stared at her two dark teeth, the only ones left in her upper jaw. She always talked about God in Polish.

"They put a crown of sharp thorns on his head and inflicted terrible wounds. The blood went pouring into his eyes."

"God does not exist. Gagarin went into space to check."

"He has punished those who check! He has sent terrible misfortunes down on them, diseases and crippled limbs!"

As she was saying this, she removed the enamel lid from the chamber pot, raised the tails of her cotton dressing gown and pissed standing up. She wasn't wearing knickers, and I could see the warm, stinky fuzz between her puckered legs.

"Would you like to play, dear?"

I exposed the black and white teeth of the piano keyboard. The instrument was out of tune, but I wasn't familiar with the correct notes. Great-Granma would sit on the bed and assume a saccharine expression, which at any moment could dissolve into tears of emotion. Sometimes she would pick up an ordinary kitchen knife from the table and scratch her back with it, with a look of sensual pleasure on her face.

I was banned from visiting Great-Granma, but if Mama wasn't at home, Aba would pretend not to know where I was.

It was Aba who had painted the portrait of Jesus in his crown of thorns: she had come up with the blood and the green hair, as well as the half-open mouth, through which I could see a gap between his front teeth. She had painted a lot of the other pictures that hung on the walls of our house.

"When I die you can take them all down to the cellar," she'd say in moments of low spirits. And I would imagine death as a cellar full of paintings.

Aba also collected albums with reproductions in them. In one of them I saw the image of a woman in an indigo dress; one of her hands was five times bigger than the other.

"Why is her hand so big?" I asked.

"That's how the artist saw it. Artists see the world differently from ordinary people."

"I'm going to be an artist too!"

"You'll be whoever you want to be!" Aba replied, and her eyes clouded with anger.

She had badly wanted to be a painter, but Great-Granma hadn't allowed her. It must have gone something like this:

"Mama, I've applied for the Academy of Fine Arts, for the graphics faculty."

"Out of the question."

"But Mama, I've already submitted my application."

"So you'll go and withdraw it."

"Mama, I am a painter. That is my vocation."

"You've no talent, you'll spend your life in poverty."

"But Mama . . . "

"End of discussion, my dear. Don't forget that during the war I gave you my last ration of bread."

In keeping with Great-Granma's plan, Aba became a doctor. Soon after she succumbed to an incurable condition affecting the joints, which meant that every movement caused her pain as sharp as the stab of a thousand knives. Just like the hand of the woman in the album, her hands were disproportionately large and swollen, in spite of which she did everything with them: she chopped vegetables and meat, she laundered the clothes and scrubbed the floor. Her face was woven from warm, transparent material, her features eluded description, and above her head, day and night, shone a slightly battered halo. Whereas her body I remember well – heavy and way-ward, it was shoddily made, like all Soviet machinery, constantly breaking down. She always spoke in Russian, although she often said: "I am Polish to the marrow of my bones."

44

Every time she said this, tears rose to her eyes, so I began to think being Polish was another sort of incurable disease, for which no drugs had been found either.

Another Pole was Tadeusz Kościuszko from the painting that hung above her bed – he and his fellow insurgents were carrying scythes with the blades pointing upwards. Also Poles were the very smart men in hats who kissed women on the hand, even a teenage girl like Aba, when she found herself in Lwów in 1944, and finally felt at home because she was in Poland. Yet in the years that followed, Poland, stylish men and all, withdrew from this city. Where did it go? Somewhere far away, across the border. Why? A mystery. Aba had stayed behind, because it hadn't taken her with it.

"If I had left, your mother wouldn't have existed, and neither would you," she consoled herself. "Or you'd have been completely different people."

When Mama grew up, she decided to become a singer, but that wasn't easy either. It went more or less like this:

"Granma, I want to apply for the conservatory."

"Out of the question."

"Granma, I've already submitted my application."

"So you'll go and withdraw it."

"Granma, I am a singer. That is my vocation."

"You've no talent, you'll spend your life in poverty."

"But Granma . . ."

"End of discussion, my dear. I've sacrificed my entire life for you – where's your gratitude?"

"I'm going to be a singer, even if you have to die first."

Great-Granma's response was to open the window and start to

scream in a shrill and sonorous voice: "Help! Save me! Call the militia! They're trying to kill me!"

But nobody reacted to her cries. Mama stuck to her guns, got into the conservatory, and stopped talking to Great-Granma.

When Aba and I went to first-night performances at the Opera, my thoughts quite often turned to suicide. Someone had told me that the architect Zygmunt Gorgolewski had killed himself when the Grand Theatre, built according to his design, began to sink and crack. Could it by chance have been retribution for the fact that Gorgolewski had buried the Poltva river underground? I thought as I walked down the central aisle, decorated with glowing carnations, symbols of the October revolution. This is where it used to flow, but he put it in a corset of stone slabs. Then they started discharging sewage into the buried river, so its corpse had gone on stinking incessantly. Beauty demands sacrifices, Aba would say, while painfully plaiting my pigtails. Was the Opera a Beauty of this kind? Had it devoured Zygmunt Gorgolewski, after he had devoured the Poltva river?

Mama was much bigger on stage than in life, and frankly speaking, she wasn't Mama. I would close my eyes to stop seeing her looking artificial in a costume, and I'd press my hands to my rib cage – her voice scrabbled at my inside. She never sang those arias at home, and so for me every performance meant rediscovering that other voice of hers again. It penetrated me, despite the shield of fingers, it made me think of the Sirens, whose singing lured sailors onto the sharp rocks. So the auditorium was a ship, the stage was the Sirens' island, I was sailing towards the rocks concealed in the orchestra pit, the powerful vibrato was speeding up the pace, and I could do nothing to resist it. The sense of imminent disaster tasted sweet, like the pink Barbarys fruitdrops I used to suck in secret, their sharp edges nicking my tongue and palate. When the ship was millimetres away from destruction, with a swift, discreet movement I would block my ears, then open my eyes and start to study the wine-red velvet on the armrests of my seat.

After the show Mama would spin in an armchair in the dressing room, wiping off her make-up, and putting Aida's diadem or Carmen's wig on my head. Off stage, her voice was still resonant. Instead of falling downwards, her short, fair, curly hair seemed to pull her head upwards, making me think she was capable of raising herself off the ground, and I imagined that when I couldn't see her, she lived in a palace of clouds and ice, just like the one the Snow Queen had.

"Did I sing well today?" she'd ask.

In response I'd pretend to be someone younger: I'd close my eyes and chew my top. Then she'd turn away from me in disgust and quiz Aba instead.

"Superbly, Marianna," she'd hear in reply. "Perfectly. Exquisitely."

I too would have liked to stand up straight and say with dignity: "Superbly. Perfectly. Exquisitely."

But that was impossible. Long ago it had come to light that I had no ear for music – I was totally tone deaf, with no hope of change. That was why the piano had been moved into Great-Granma's room – which I wasn't allowed to enter. I had to go underground with my plonking on the ivories, just like the Poltva river. I was unworthy of the Opera, unworthy of the first-night shows, unworthy of Mama. I wanted to go home.

*

The topography of our flat was fixed for good: just as the seas, mountains and deserts never change their position on the map, so the position of the furniture, fittings and domestic appliances was immovable in our house. This permanence of objects was probably a response to the instability of human fate. Great-Granma's husband, and thus my great-grandfather, was arrested in Leningrad in 1937 during the "Polish operation", Stalin's purge of Poles, and then vanished for ever. Aba's husband, and thus my grandfather, had survived the entire war with the rank of officer in the Red Army, finally reaching Berlin, and then died in the mid-1960s as a result of what nowadays we would call chronic depression combined with cirrhosis of the liver. As for my father, I doubted he really existed.

I was the fruit of a short-lived, poetic romance that happened in the summer of 1975. On June 1 my parents – Mama was in her final year as a student in the voice faculty, and my father was a young architect from Moscow – met at a party, and then for an entire month, night after night, they recited Russian poetry of the Silver Age to each other from memory. Mama knew Tsvetaeva best of all, and my father's favourite was definitely Blok. As legend has it, they didn't miss a single night. I don't know if they had to learn new poems during the day; perhaps their existing reserves of poetry were rich enough. But you would have to know a huge number of poems to suffice for thirty nights on end. I don't know if Tsvetaeva and Blok actually wrote that many. That summer Aba and Great-Granma were on holiday by the Black Sea, allowing the poetry marathon to which I owe my life to take place at our flat.

My parents met for the last time on June 30, on a platform at the main railway station. The Lvov–Moscow train was shuddering from the actions of a railway worker checking the condition of the carriages, the fertilised egg cell was quivering inside my mother, and my father was trembling with emotion. Their parting words to each other were straight out of Mayakovsky:

"Listen! If stars are lit, does it mean there's someone who needs them?" Mama asked.

"It means that for someone those specks of spit are like pearls," my father shouted back, as the locomotive slowly began to move. They never saw each other again.

The first time I made my presence known was on the day before Mama's final exam; she was ironing a white nylon shirt when the world went spinning before her eyes. The cruel toxicosis at the start of her pregnancy was mistaken for ordinary food poisoning, and for a long time after that it was thought to be a symptom of some other chronic illness.

It wouldn't have been any trouble to have me aborted, but Mama's response was an adamant no. All the arguments about wasting her start in life were to no avail. Nor did she inform my father. As she later explained, she didn't want prose to encroach on their poetry. And every decision that Mama made was immovable, like a rock.

So when the snow was melting, and the old women were coming out on the city streets to sell the little heads of sheltered crocuses stored in the palms of their hands, I was brought home. According to family folklore it was the first real day of spring, a deluge of warmth and light. As though the sun had burst into the flat for an inspection, ready to illuminate everything, even the least visible speck on the windowpanes, yet they'd been washed to perfection for my arrival. By contrast, the stained-glass window on our stairwell had to wait for years before someone came along with a cloth and gave it a thorough cleaning.

Much later on, I discovered that not every house has a stained-glass window hidden inside, and if it does have one, it's much smaller. Ours occupied the entire stairwell. Like a stage curtain it separated the interior of the house from the yard outside, extending across every floor from top to bottom, or maybe vice versa – from bottom to top. We lived on the first floor, and we only had to open the door to see its middle section: the remains of a brown-and-fiery underworld, out of which grew the long, solitary trunk of a tree, cutting a turquoise lake in half. The neighbours who lived above us could see the opposite shore, on which rose green mountains and blue pines. Anyone who climbed to the attic saw them pass into the white and lilac of the clouds. Our downstairs neighbour, crazy Luba, could see nothing – the lowest part of the window had been lost long ago, and in its place some transparent panes had been installed, exposing our cramped inner yard. The caretaker and her numerous children viewed the stained-glass window from this perspective. Every morning one of them would appear by the sewage grate with a large bucket to be emptied and stop there, with its eyes raised to the underside of the window, which was grey and bulging.

"They have no household amenities," Aba would say in a tone that was more of condemnation than sympathy.

The Stained-Glass Window 1

I had no memory of Mykola from the days of my childhood, so I think of the day when the stained-glass window had its bath as our first encounter. It happened one autumn in the mid-1990s. Its harbingers were some unwelcome visitors on our stairwell.

They would appear at night, and they weren't deterred by the new door code – evidently they knew the combination. They drank colourless liquid from plastic bottles, which they left crumpled on the stairs, and tossed about dog-ends smoked down to the filter. Sometimes we could hear them performing Nirvana songs on a guitar. They'd piss in corners of the courtyard. They ran off if Luba went into action armed with a scrubbing brush. Once in a while she would go to the militia station across the street to report them.

"They're making a mess!" she'd shriek. "They're drug addicts! It's antisocial behaviour!"

The guardians of law and order, in their creased blue shirts with crookedly attached epaulettes, would stand under our balcony during cigarette breaks that lasted for hours. They had the sad faces of shepherds uprooted from their native Carpathians, they'd agree with Luba, spit on the ground and litter the pavement with trampled butts from the same kind of cigarettes the nocturnal visitors smoked. They had their reasons for not taking any action.

After each night-time visit a piece of glass or two would be missing from the window.

Barbarians, I fumed with rage. They're filling their tatty pockets with a work of art. They're doing it for entertainment. Soon they'll take the whole thing away, and then what shall we do?

One night Aba went out to confront them in her dressing gown.

"A masterpiece!" I heard among the isolated words that reached me. "Unique! A hundred years old! Irretrievably and for ever!"

Just like the militiamen, the young people nodded indifferently, with a hint of nostalgia, but after this incident the pieces of glass stopped vanishing – the company moved on to somewhere else. Yet a sense of threat still emanated from the holes left by the stolen pieces.

A few months later some new visitors appeared in the house. These ones came in the daytime. They had cameras, they took pictures, measured the stained-glass window and made some drawings on sheets of paperboard spread out on the windowsill. I was more afraid of them than of their predecessors. They looked like academics, and that did not bode well. They've persuaded the city council to give them illicit permission to dismantle the window, I thought in horror – they're planning to take it away to some museum in Kiev, it'll fall apart during transportation, and then our entire house will collapse, because nobody can possibly survive an operation that cuts out their heart. Luba kept a passive eye on the newcomers, because they weren't making a mess.

"Do you people have permission for your research?" Aba asked one day, unable to stop herself.

She was answered by a tall, middle-aged man who seemed to be in charge of the rest. His voice was so soft I could barely hear him, though I had pressed myself bodily to the peephole.

"It's nothing to be worried about, we're just documenting the window on behalf of the glass department at the Lviv Fine Arts Academy. We're registering each section. We want to do it before it's too late."

Too late? How did he dare to use that phrase?

"Oh hello, I didn't recognise you," said Aba, suddenly changing her tone.

I took a careful look at him: tall, with long hair. I wonder why I don't have tutors like that? I thought. Mine wore rumpled clothes and looked as though they had ended up at the academy by accident. This one seemed ready to stake his life on his every word. Perhaps he had already done it, by laying it on some altar unknown to me.

I was still standing by the peephole. Aba suggested that he should come in for a cup of tea, but he declined.

As he was passing our door on his way upstairs, I glanced at his shoes. Leather, and unnaturally long; once they had stretched their tentacles half way across the hallway, they continued to grow on the striped doormat for ages, frightening me with their undeniable masculinity. Shoes from years ago.

Next day he came in tennis shoes and sportswear, and out of a large bag he fetched some rags and a bucket. He rang at our door.

"May I please trouble you for some water?"

I showed him to the bathroom and back again, left the door to the flat ajar, and watched as he made foam appear in the bucket and started to wash the stained-glass window. He had a long stick, which he used to reach the most inaccessible parts. I know that this time Luba was watching him through her peephole.

I was standing on the threshold as he scrubbed the white and lilac clouds and the summits of the mountains. I was sitting on the stairs when the soapy rivers ran into the blue of the lake. I was by the windowsill when the sloping roofs of the cabins scattered on the hillsides turned out to be tinged bright yellow, and not in the least bit emerald, as I had always thought. I was holding the bucket when his long fingers began to remove the dirt caked among the roots of the brown tree. They were the same height, he and the glass oak, they wrestled like two colossi, they fought over who could block out more of the sunlight that had suddenly flooded the entire stairwell, and it occurred to me that a small, but resonant organ would be a good thing to have in this doorway. I washed the plain glass opposite Luba's door myself, trying not to betray the fact that I had never washed a single window in my life before.

"I wonder what the people feel when they dust Michelangelo's 'Pietà'?" I said later, when he came in for a cup of tea. Aba wasn't at home, and Great-Granma was hiding in her room.

"I haven't been here for ages – nothing has changed," he replied at a tangent.

A thread of grey shone in his hair as it gently fell to his shoulders. In his left ear he had a tiny earring – an unheard-of extravagance in those days.

"I feel as though someone has washed the windscreen of the car I'm riding in."

"And I feel as though someone has turned back time," he said, smiling, as he looked through Mama's collection of L.P.s. "I brought most of these records here once upon a time."

Soon after, we went back to the stairwell to enjoy the reclaimed colours.

"I've searched everywhere, in this city and abroad, but this window is one of a kind. Here and there you find small stained-glass windows, but not an eleven-metre gap in the fabric of the building. It's the house that was made to fit the window, not the other way around."

I shuddered – I had always wanted to know something about the stained-glass window.

"As for the colours," he went on, "I've counted seventy-two of them. In the Middle Ages they used about ten. This is pure Impressionism. Unfortunately nobody knows who created it." He raised his voice a little, because I was standing on the next landing up. "They don't know anything about it at the Żeleński glassworks in Kraków, where most of this city's stained-glass windows were made before the war.

"Earth, water, sky – the picture develops by theme from bottom to top. The lowest part, the underworld, is missing – nobody knows what's happened to it. This window is an allegory for life's upward climb. It accompanies anyone who goes up or down the winding stairs."

"Where could I attend your lectures?" I asked, but he didn't answer. He took his rags and bucket and went on his way without saying goodbye. I went back into the flat and jotted down everything I'd heard him say.

Aida

Later on, once a great deal had happened between us, Mykola yielded to my requests and told me about his first evening with Mama. Not about the first time he saw her, but about the day when he'd realised he loved her. It happened early in the spring of 1986, during "Aida", when suddenly, in the middle of the show, a man in the audience died.

For Mykola it was yet another evening when he had found an excuse to go to the theatre after work. Holding an old leather bag, in the final minutes before the curtain went up, he had entered the packed-out auditorium; on the way he had kissed the hand of Nilovna, the elderly usherette in a navy-blue suit, whose tall hair and noble profile heralded the imminent appearance on stage of a litter with a battered sphinx on its side. Mykola had picked out a seat in the third row, and the man had been sitting in the second.

That evening was the first when Mykola admitted to himself that Marianna's voice had a curious effect on him; it seemed to open a long-forgotten door inside him. On the other side of it were the Carpathians, Hrebenne – his mother's family village, a shepherd in rubber boots, milk straight from the cow, and above all the swing, too big for the little boy he had been then. When he swung way up high, right over the mountains, time and thought disappeared, releasing his awareness of being alive – the pure, ontological essence of existence that neither now, nor then was he capable of naming. As an adult he had felt it again every time he heard Marianna's mezzo soprano voice. So when the first notes of "Aida" resounded, his inner eye could see a desirable, distant reality, while with the flair of a professional his corporeal eyes were taking note of the theatrical facts: the deficiencies of the old-fashioned set, the anachronistic features of the costumes, and especially the ugliness of Amneris' dress – he knew that responsibility for its dirty-green colour lay with the Communist Party.

Whenever the soloists fell silent and the choir came in, Mykola imagined a river full of fish. Large and small, they were moving about at variable speeds and at various depths. The visible ones near the surface were lit up by the sun, and they were the sopranos. Beneath them bigger, darker fish wound their way like a ribbon – the altos. The bed of the river was covered in slow, heavy fish with long whiskers, impossible to distinguish from the silty sand – the bass singers. The tenors were imperceptible. As he waited for Amneris' next appearance, Mykola remembered what was in his bag – a bottle of dry Tokaj, which he had received as a gift just before the show.

Towards the end of the second act, when the Pharaoh betroths his daughter Amneris to Radames, and she starts to enjoy a moment of triumph, something unexpected happened. The head directly in front of Mykola, which he hadn't really noticed before because it didn't stick out above the rest, swayed first to the right, then to the left, and finally sank downwards. The women sitting on either side leaned over the man, and then one of them screamed: "Fetch a doctor!"

Mykola rushed to find Nilovna, who put on the lights in the auditorium; Marianna's voice shuddered, she emitted two wrong notes and fell silent. For a while the orchestra went on playing as though nothing were wrong, but then it dried up too. A doctor was found among the audience. After a short examination he asked Mykola to help him carry the body into the corridor. The painted curtain came down halfway. A murmur ran through the auditorium: "Ruptured aorta."

In the poorly lit foyer Mykola found a telephone, dialled the emergency number 03, and asked for an ambulance. The stiffening body in an ill-fitting suit lay quite near the grand staircase, with Nilovna watching over it and chasing away the gawkers. Mykola couldn't tear his gaze from the horn-rimmed spectacles, fastened with a bit of string on one side – they lay at an angle across the face with its eyes closed. It was clear the owner would never be needing them again.

He and the doctor went outside; neither of them put on a coat, but both took out cigarettes and matches. It was drizzling; under the chestnut trees the light from the elegant lamps trembled, and there was hardly a soul about.

"Maybe we should cover him up?"

The doctor, a slender man with a grey moustache, waved a hand dismissively.

"I'd like to die at that speed too – one, two, three, bang!" he admitted with a sigh.

"He didn't look old," said Mykola.

"Fifty-six," replied the doctor, and showed him the dead man's passport. "Luckily he had it on him."

Twenty-eight plus twenty-eight is fifty-six – I'm exactly half way through life, thought Mykola, as he leafed through the passport of Andrei Andreyevich Fetisov. This alarming calculation remained with him until the very end of that long and eventful evening.

As the show continued, Mykola and the doctor had time to discuss a few things and freeze to the bone, but the ambulance still wasn't there. It appeared shortly before the spectators filled the square in front of the theatre. They were laughing and chatting, smoking and spitting as ever – there was nothing to imply that anyone was still thinking about the incident. Evidently Fetisov had come to hear "Aida" on his own.

After completing his mission, Mykola went back into the theatre. He exchanged a few words with Nilovna, cast a glance at the empty spot near the grand staircase and went down to the dressing rooms. He already knew which door to knock at – that voice came echoing off the walls and showed him the way.

"I got the most awful fright! I sang off-key!" she said in despair, sitting before a triple mirror; lying unbuttoned on top of tubes of make-up, the dirty-green dress resembled the open belly of a gutted trout. A make-up girl was helping Marianna to tidy her hair. Not so long ago the whole theatre had been gossiping about the story of that dress: like every Soviet show before its premiere, the new staging of "Aida" had to be approved by a committee formed of a wide circle of Communist Party women – old bags who sniffed out hidden anti-regime allusions and other expressions of dissent. This time they had latched onto Amneris' dress – the director had intended it to be blue like the Mediterranean and gold like ancient Egyptian women's decorations. A highly suspect colour scheme! Anyone should understand that in this city not even the Pharaoh's daughter could appear in something like that.

"Excuse me," Mykola said. He stood in the entrance, without closing the door behind him. He had only talked to Marianna in person once before: the lighting technician had introduced them in the buffet. Charming woman, cold bitch, he had warned Mykola as they were approaching her table.

"I hear you helped out with all the ghastly horror," she said, lowering her voice, as she spun her chair around and stretched out both hands to him. Mykola sensed the theatricality of this gesture, but without a moment's hesitation he stepped forward to reciprocate, and even touched her ice-cold palms to his chest. The make-up girl vanished.

Marianna's fingers showed surprising agility, and finally it was she who opened the Tokaj. They tried using a pen, a bradawl, a screwdriver and some keys – the eventual winner was a key, her short, strong key to the front door. It had an unusual oval tip which helped to push the cork inside the bottle without breaking it in the process. They were sitting in the Zankovetska theatre café, opening the wine under the table – this story is set in the dismal years of Gorbachev's anti-alcohol campaign – and now and then their fingers collided. They had ordered so-called cocktails: grape juice with a scoop of melted ice cream. They were alone in the room; the Soviet pop star Alla Pugacheva's hits played in the background, as a fat old hag with a white cap pinned to her hair watched them through drooping, drunken eyes from behind the counter. It didn't matter – Marianna had insisted on leaving the Opera as fast as possible and doing something that would help her to get over the death in the auditorium.

She talked non-stop. About tonight's incident and about productions of "Aida" at other theatres, about the tough time Nilovna had had in the war and the murmuring of the underground river that was audible in some corners of the Opera, and Mykola discovered that every one of the themes she brought up with invariable ardour acted on him in the same way as her singing – it was like Christ's call to Lazarus. Tremors he had never felt before were running down the back of his neck and then branching off in various directions, reanimating various parts of his body: suddenly he became aware of having ankles and toes, lungs and ribs, an Adam's apple and cheek bones, wrists and a solar plexus. Warmth strayed up and down his torso, as though someone had wound him in a net of sunbeams; his only concern was that the wet stains under his arms might be showing, as he went on pouring the wine beneath the table into glasses streaked with "cocktail". The final topic, the link between the Opera and the underground river, particularly intrigued Marianna.

"There's no doubt at all: some members of the orchestra can hear it," she said. "And I can't stop thinking about it."

Mykola unsteadily approached the bar, asked for a glass and poured some Tokaj for the woman in the cap. She hawked up a thank you, knocked the wine back like vodka, switched off Pugacheva and disappeared behind the scenes.

"I imagined Andrei Andreyevich and those lifeless spectacles of his being carried down the Poltva by Charon with the face of Nilovna," he said as he returned to Marianna.

Her brow is furrowed with wrinkles – not surprising for someone with such lively facial expressions, he thought, and her fair, wavy hair crowns her with a coiffure more triumphal than any diadem. An amphora, he thought next, she's an amphora full of mysterious liquid, and somehow I seem to be dying of thirst.

There was no rational reason why they didn't finish the bottle in the café, but tried to carry it upright in his bag; in fact it was he who made the attempt, while she just occasionally nudged it with a gloveless hand; together they considered the fate of the cork trapped inside – there was no force on earth that could have extracted it without breaking the glass. They walked in no particular direction, letting their coat sleeves brush against each other with the ease of long-time lovers, and making jokes about people coming to sudden ends at the theatre.

"Will you come down into the vaults of the Opera with me?" asked Marianna, once they were sitting on a small, wet bench in Kościuszko Park.

"Pioneer's word of honour," replied Mykola, as he fetched out the Tokaj and took a swig. Just then the nearest bushes moved, two men emerged from them, and Marianna sent a scream halfway across the park.

"Volunteer militia," said the men and showed their I.D. cards. "There's no need to shout, dear citizen. Your documents, please."

At once she had realised what was in the wind: consumption of alcoholic beverages in a park meant a fine, your workplace would be notified, and would hold meetings, both Party and Union, to discuss your case. Breaking the anti-alcohol decree issued by the Soviet Communist Party Central Committee meant a reprimand entered in the files and the loss of your annual bonus.

And the whole theatre gossiping about my night with the young set designer, it then occurred to her.

Mykola stared at the volunteer militiaman's I.D. card in dismay – it revealed that he too was called Andrei Andreyevich.

"Comrade!" cried Marianna. "Have you ever been in love? So deeply that it makes you sweat in the winter, so deeply that your whole body is alive, aching with life, and your throat sings beautiful arias?"

"No," replied the volunteer, though his tone implied hesitation.

"I love this man. I love him to death, and with all my life. It only dawned on me today. So we wanted to celebrate. To prove it, I'll sing for you."

Marianna stood up and softly began to croon "Moscow Nights".

The man called Andrei Andreyevich stood next to her and listened, while the other one chatted with Mykola. Marianna was never to find out what they had discussed, or that the guardian of public order had been won over by a method that we might call passing a twenty-five rouble note from one hand to another on the quiet.

The last stop that evening was the front entrance of the house where Marianna lived. Tired, they stood in the dark on the ground floor; the light bulb on the stairwell had just burned out.

"But you went over the top about love," said Mykola softly. He felt disenchanted and disgusted by the incident in the park. He had been hoping for something quite different: he was going to tell her how he'd found the boxes in the attic of the villa on Leo Tolstoy Street, and he was going to kiss her. But now he was gripped by cold, and felt his entire body weaken.

Marianna replied with such a loud burst of laughter that the floor behind the door of the nearest flat creaked and someone evidently came up to the peephole.

"Music is what really moves me. It surprises me, because I'm cold-blooded and my nerves are as strong as steel." After a pause she added: "That was a quote from the letters of Solomiya Krushelnytska. Have you read them?"

Mykola didn't answer.

"Going back to the stained-glass window. Nobody knows who made it or when. It's a total enigma, one of the many in this city. I have no idea where to find information about it. I've never shown it to anyone in the dark before. Don't you think that's a distinction for you and your talents," she stated, rather than asked, and then pressed her lips to his. During this kiss both their mouths remained closed. Then she took his hand in hers and laid it on the glass.

"The four elements are depicted here. Starting from the top: air, earth, water and fire. You have your hand on the fire. It's the only part that hasn't survived."

The window was icy, and Mykola quickly withdrew his hand – suddenly he felt as though it would freeze to the glass and he'd have to stay in this entrance for ever. He left without saying goodbye and quickly turned into Akademitska.

Akademitska

The street that began just around the corner from our flat was known to us as Akademitska, although the signs showed another name: Taras Shevchenko Avenue. It had three cinemas, lots of shops and an avenue of tall poplar trees down the middle, along which the Poltva river had once flowed. Every few days Aba and I flowed along it too, very slowly, unfortunately. Now and then we had to drop anchor in a port, meaning a shop, and that was the whole principle of the task I hated most as a child: going shopping.

Akademitska Street started at the square where the sculpted armchair of the Polish playwright Aleksander Fredro had once stood, with Fredro himself sitting in it, but in our day, there was no armchair and nobody to sit in it, just pigeons swaying on the heavy chains bordering the square; each link ended in a stone ball with spikes sticking out of it. The arms race, I thought, every time I looked at them.

Akademitska Street also meant the corner building, and in it the cinema named after the revolutionary Mykola Shchors; beside it stood a soda-water vending machine, into which you had to toss a coin, and then from the top of a little window the liquid jetted into a thick glass; after drinking you were meant to turn it upside down and rinse it out in water spurting from the bottom. In the early 1990s chains were fitted to the glasses, and towards the end of the decade the machines were jettisoned, but right now I'm talking about the 1980s.

On hand-painted posters I read: "Andrei Tarkovsky's 'Nostalgia'". Outside the cinema a queue had formed that ran halfway down the street.

"What is nostalgia?" I asked Aba.

"Longing for your homeland," she replied, and stared into space. I don't know if she was thinking of Leningrad–St Petersburg, where she was born and had lived before the war, or of Poland, which had always been her dream, and which had cleared off out of this city.

Past the cinema was a shop called "Galanteria" – meaning "Accessories" – which smelled of perfume and sweat. I couldn't understand what we went in there for, since we never intended to buy anything, but I'd meekly follow Aba, trying not to breathe through my nose. There were glass display cases with open lipsticks standing like rockets ready for take-off, and powder compacts driving along like tanks, beside menacing nail-polish bazookas, black umbrella radar dishes and parachute-like bras. There was a crush and a clamour, as portly ladies pushed towards the counter, unashamedly extracting their beige bosoms from their dresses to try on the bras; meanwhile the counter bristled with men's fake black leather gloves, and I thought that any moment now they'd reach for the women's flabby skin, their yelling throats, their flaccid nipples, and attack. Indeed the women walking along Akademitska were repugnant: they trailed bags of shopping and grizzly children behind them, they dripped sweat and mooed at each other. The men were quite another matter – cleaner and quieter, they plodded along heavily, dressed in indistinguishable grey overcoats and hats with small brims, which they raised in a dignified way whenever they ran into an acquaintance.

On Akademitska was the café Snihurochka – the "Snow Maiden" – with two identical dining rooms in two neighbouring houses; a pair of identical twins with purple hair were the waitresses there, serving Plombir ice cream in little metal bowls, to which you could add jam, cocoa or walnuts as you wished.

I liked the shop called "Hlib", the Ukrainian for bread, and its sales ladies with ruddy cheeks and hair tucked into snow-white bonnets. They never shouted, they reminded me of attentive doctors – in fact they were more important, because they provided bread, and not so very long ago people had been starving to death. We would buy a white cob and half a loaf of rye, we would buy crescent-shaped buns for six *kopecks* and small spherical rolls for three; I would stuff myself with them along the way. Hlib also had a confectionery department, which was usually empty; only rarely would the round shape of a cake or two appear in a corner of the display case, and then a queue of shrewd ladies would quickly form, and there would be nothing left again. We were not shrewd, so I could only dream of cake, such as the kind with the Town Hall drawn in cocoa powder on a creamy-white background and the blurred inscription "Lvov", that looked as though it had been dusted in sweet snow.

"That cream is made with margarine," said Aba to console me. I knew that you could buy margarine without queuing; it smelled inedible, so adding it to the "Lvov" cake was an act of profanity and sabotage.

Past Hlib came a shop called "Kovbasa" – "Sausage". Before going in I would lay my hands on my chest to protect myself from being trampled by the crowd. Inside there were three queues; the difference between them wasn't clear, and we'd take our places in two parallel lines, because one might move faster than the other. The crowd would sway, push and shove me from one place to the next, as I caught the scent of Astrakhan sheepskins and woollen coats, giving me a close-up view of briefcases with combination locks, dirty string shopping bags and little dogs on leads. Here the sales assistants were as inaccessible and implacable as queens; their ample figures were too big for their frilly aprons – they'd eaten too much *kovbasa*, gobbling it down like pigs – after all, they didn't have to kill themselves standing in line. They cheated on the weight, hid goods under the counter for their friends, and said to the rest: "*Nema i nie bulo*" – "There isn't any, and there never was". They were like the slave traders in *Uncle Tom's Cabin* – all they lacked were the whips. As the shop creaked at the seams, I longed for the customers to rebel against their rule, to start a revolution, for us to charge at them in unison, knock them off their throne, take all the *kovbasa*, share it out fraternally, then quickly disperse and go home. Instead, we went on waiting doggedly, each in our own place. Today, as a rare exception, they had butter on offer too, so my presence was essential – they were providing two hundred grams per person, and there were entire families standing in line to get the extra rations. My queue moved faster than Aba's, I had now reached the counter and had pressed my forehead against it, afraid it would crack under my weight, so forceful was the pressure from behind. Only now could I finally see the enamel trays with cobblestone-like chunks of Soviet *mortadela* of various kinds: with large or small lumps of fat, and smooth, with no fat at all. I was so near our goal, yet I still felt anxious lest the people in front of us took too much, or the sales assistants cried out: "*Skinchylos!*" – "All gone!", while pointedly tossing the final piece onto a large metal scale. But we made it, and our portion was wrapped in stiff paper – at once some dark stains spread across it. We pushed our way towards the exit: mind the child please, carefully now – could you get off my foot, madam? What an ill-mannered person! How uncouth! I was clearing myself a path, with my fists pressed to my rib cage, when suddenly at the back of the queue I saw Great-Granma. Aba cast her a casual "Hello" and kept moving, but I was halted in my tracks, alarmed by the contrast between her familiar, at-home face and her outdoor clothes, the hat covering her sparse white hair and the beautiful velour coat with an amber butterfly pinned to the collar. Was this really the woman I ran into every day on the route between the bathroom and her bedroom? Was this the woman who went about in her dressing gown and publicly pissed in a chamber pot? Here, among strangers, she looked like the refined heroine of a film, and Aba's dry, official greeting intensified that impression even more.

"Why does Great-Granma have to stand in the same queue a second time?" I asked when we got outside.

Aba's answer was not immediate.

"After she and your mother quarrelled we started to run separate households."

In the virulent tone in which she spoke about events from before my birth, I perceived something like a sense of guilt.

We walked on, to the shop called "Tiutiun" – meaning "Tobacco", sent there by Mama's secret habit, which we weren't allowed to mention to anyone and which Aba claimed would deprive her of her voice and cut short her singing career. The ceiling and walls were covered with the figures of Cossacks, half-recumbent in close ranks beside their horses, amid the fumes of their own pipes; their fine dark eyes were closed, the feet emerging from their dark-blue pantaloons were long, their nails clipped, and their wavy topknots grew into their horses' curly manes. In this shop the sales girls were dozy too; on the counters lay nothing but blue-and-white packets of Belomorkanal, the unfiltered cigarettes smoked by workmen on building sites, but we were looking for the Orbit brand for Mama, which that particular day was "off".

Next came "Ryba" – "Fish". Outside the shop stood a wet truck, and beside it a sad man in a dark blue apron, with the eyes and whiskers of the Cossacks from the Tiutiun ceiling, would be fishing out live carp with a net and serving them to the women in the queue. Once we bought one of those carp, and it swam about in our bathtub, as pink as the lady with the large hand in Matisse's painting – you only had to pull out the plug to rob it of its life.

In a shop called "Svitoch" – meaning "Torch" – where despite the large windows not much light got in, the counters were laden with loose sweets and so-called "chocolate-like products". It always smelled of cigarettes in there; the smoke climbed up the stairs and coiled around the potted ficus plants like grey cotton wool. We would buy pink Barbarys fruit drops, and I'd never so much as glance towards the stairs; I was afraid that as soon as I stepped any closer I'd be swept down a chasm like Káča, the girl in the Czech folk tale who made a pact with the devil. Aba had told me that down in Svitoch's basement there was a drinking den. People with jobs do not frequent such places – the men who sit there are layabouts and alcoholics, they smoke and drink, and there are women among them too. There's nothing worse in the world than a woman who has gone to the dogs. By their very nature women are wiser, finer-looking and smarter than men, which is why the fall of such a creature is much worse than the degradation of an animal that's less sharp-witted by nature; in other words – a man, Aba explained to me. Sometimes there were fallen women perched on the railings outside the door to the Svitoch shop; they had puffy eyes, garish make-up and bizarre messy hairdos. I don't know why they always wore trousers, by contrast with Aba and other women with jobs, who invariably dressed in mid-length dark skirts. In the fallen women's exaggerated gestures and husky voices there was a sense of freedom and nonchalance that the women with jobs had never known. They were alluring and evil all at once, like the tigers prowling behind the bars of their cages at the zoo.

At the end of Akademitska there was a large grocery store, known colloquially as "the Passage", because you could walk right through it. The counters were glaringly empty, the fat sales ladies, lacking the glamour of *kovbasa*, were like sea lions tossed ashore – dealing in matches, buckwheat and powdered puddings didn't provide much inspiration. From there we would turn towards the Ukraina cinema, which was also showing "Nostalgia"; the information painted on the posters was in a different hand. Through the open door into the foyer we could see the flashing red and green lights of fruit machines. Like the Shchors, the Ukraina was in a corner building, and above the entrance I could see a carved medallion with a quote from Lenin: "Art belongs to the people". Who else could it belong to? I thought in amazement. Here Akademitska came to an end; I turned to look back, and a little way off I saw Great-Granma coming after us.

"Why do we still live with her?" I asked.

"You have no idea what the housing problem is like!" said Aba irritably. "How the hell would we get separate flats?"

Her irritation suggested to me that in fact Aba *wanted* to live with Great-Granma, even though she didn't like her.

Located a little further on, Halytska Square had a high, wrought-iron gate, but how on earth could something like that hold back the flood of the bazaar that came gushing through the holes in its lacy weave, pouring into the nearest side streets in the form of cactuses in pots and illicit snowdrops, and the baby-like squealing of pigs to be slaughtered and transported in zipped-up bags on wheels? On the square, there were shop signs featuring foodstuffs in sight, no price lists or queues, and nobody called each other "comrade", but "sir" and "madam" were heard, forms of address that had only survived in the countryside. Coming into the city from their villages, the tradeswomen stood on makeshift platforms above heaps of potatoes and carrots, eggs and meat, shouting and gesticulating, unashamed of their fat, blackened fingers. They were not horrified, as I was, by the lifeless pig's trotters, they'd slice off thick chunks of white cheese and pass them to me to try, open bottles of sunflower oil and generously pour it into my hand. The tradeswomen wore headscarves and the customers hats, the village women spoke only in Ukrainian, the city ladies in Ukrainian and Russian. At the bazaar, everything was very expensive, so Aba would haggle, and we only ever bought boring things, such as beetroots and potatoes. Finally we'd go inside the covered part, where there were none of our local traders; instead, there were gentlemen with dark stubble and heavy accents, in large, grey flat caps. They stood on platforms too, but the heaps that rose before them were from under a different sun – from Georgia and Armenia they brought pomegranates and oranges, lemons and persimmons. It was mainly gentlemen in hats who bought their produce; they'd open their briefcases with combination locks, carefully store bulging packages inside, and then slowly lock them. I saw this gesture as an indirect confession to a crime, for as everyone knew, life wasn't meant to be like that: all citizens were supposed to be equal, with just as many rights and responsibilities, just as many oranges and apricots, but it turned out quite differently. We could afford hardly a thing, while they could afford everything.

"When we were evacuated to Kazan during the war, Great-Granma gave her bread ration to me," Aba said suddenly. "I was constantly hungry because I was growing," she added after a pause. "I used to have dreams about the crusts of bread I'd hidden under the edges of my plate before the war."

I turned to take another look at Great-Granma in her coat and hat. On one occasion I'd been greatly surprised when she had shown me some photographs taken in her youth, in which she was wearing various carnival costumes – a sort of turban with a feather, a dress patterned with stars and some elegant harem pants. As she told me about her favourite costume balls, she came to life; she described the fabric and cut of those outfits in detail, and in a hushed voice admitted that one New Year's Eve the candles decorating the

Christmas tree had set the train of her dress on fire, and it was a miracle that she hadn't been burned – that had been before the war, in Leningrad. As she said all this, she kept raising her hands to her hair, as though adjusting an elegant coiffure. In fact, by contrast with the rest of her body, she always took care of her hair and fingernails – she regularly went to a hairdresser, who cut her hair in a bob, and then she would shave the fine hairs on her neck herself with a razor. Once when I was smaller, I had mistaken this razor for a nail file, and had cut my fingers – the blood had streamed out in a broad trickle, like Jesus' in the picture. As a result, Mama found out that I'd been breaking her rule, and was extremely angry with me. But I still felt drawn to Great-Granma's dark den and the piano.

Laden with shopping bags, we were walking home along the middle of Akademitska, without going into any more shops, and yet to my mind we were walking too slowly, stopping at intervals under each successive poplar tree.

"Why are we trailing along like tortoises?" I asked in a raised voice, to my own surprise. "Why can't you walk as fast as I can?" I went on after a pause, because Aba hadn't reacted. "I know you're sick. But what's wrong with you? Tell me, why are you like this?"

She still did not answer, which meant that I had crossed a line that shouldn't be crossed, I had asked a question that shouldn't be asked, I had spoken words that shouldn't be spoken, but it was impossible to take them back – words emerge winged but come back hooved. I had burned my bridges behind me for good and all.

"I'm not going to drag along after you!" I said. "I can't stand it! I want to run around! I'm sick of all these shopping bags!"

I turned away and marched on ahead. She remained alone, silent and indifferent, while I ran; soon I was at the end of the avenue, or maybe the beginning, depending which direction you were facing. I hopped up and down on one leg, feeling worse and worse. I didn't stop watching Aba furtively, I could see her bandy legs in their darned stockings, and the cluster of string bags encircling her, which she wasn't capable of carrying; there were jars and sausage sticking out of them. If only she were free and without cares, I thought, instead of slow and sick. If only she did something other than shopping and cooking, if only she'd stop tormenting me. I knew these were nasty thoughts that I should never entertain, but what was I to do, when they sprang up in me of their own accord? And if so, then I must be a nasty person, tough luck, I couldn't back out of my nastiness now, it had already taken hold of me, I had already strayed too far from the straight and narrow, but at the same time I had nowhere to go, and there was nobody waiting for me at home. So I stood still on the lawn instead of Fredro, whom the Poles from Poland had taken off to their country, and gazed in the direction of the Shchors cinema – the queue had disbanded, the film had been running for ages. I fed the pigeons the remains of my crescent roll, and swung on the spiked chains. Aba must have run into Great-Granma, who would be helping her – so what if she was older? More importantly she was healthy, so they'd manage to toddle home together. But I decided to stay there on my own until evening; I had just realised that I was a bad girl, and bad children are bound to remain alone.

The Italian Courtyard

We never ran into each other in the dust-coated corridors of the Academy of Fine Arts, where he taught and I studied, but I started meeting him in the city centre. Both of us were products of Lviv, an egg incubated by this city, we had hatched out on its streets and were inscribed into them: he was the spiked halo of the Pensive Christ on top of the Boim Chapel, I was the head of a lion carved on its base, he was the cracked steps leading into the Dominican church, I was the polished, pine-cone shaped knob on the door of a Renaissance house, he was the cobbled surface of Pekarska Street, I was the clapper in the Korniakt Tower bell, still silenced until recently. We had always walked these same streets, but only now did we start to recognise each other – good day, hello, and how are you, what's new? Admiringly, I watched the effort he made to keep his head high though burdened with sorrows; it seemed to me to be bursting with noble cares that would have been beyond the strength of the average person. He led me here and there, showing me ugly memorial plaques that had freshly appeared on beautiful houses, criticised the configuration of the new monuments and praised the old sculptors' perfect knowledge of anatomy. I had always tried my best to read the city like a great book, but it turned out he was the one who knew its alphabet. As we stood outside a house that had recently cast off its plaster, he said: "This is in Yiddish: 'coffee, tea, milk'. Every spring the city moults, revealing letters from various scripts on its façades. The present authorities treat this occurrence like a dangerous disease. Something like a rash. Eradicated in one place, the symptoms keep appearing in others. Yet the self-taught doctors are sure of their qualifications and their chosen therapy."

"And it never works?"

"Not so far. But . . . it'll soon be over. For me, the stained-glass window on your stairwell is the city's final cultural membrane. If that tears, nothing is going to save it."

"The fall of Rome?" I suggested hesitantly.

He looked at me piercingly, maybe too much so, and that penetrating gaze began to frighten me. I glanced at his hands – the wedding ring on his finger was like a declaration of my untouchability. While his eyes caressed the vestiges of Jewish life as tenderly as they did the glass tree in our stairwell, I dropped my gaze to his old lace-up shoes, black and shiny like a sheet of vinyl recording the best operatic performances, which nobody in our house had listened to for years.

"Where can I catch your lectures?" I asked, but he pretended not to hear me, and vanished back into his all-knowing sorrows, to which I had no admission.

"Meet me for coffee tomorrow at four, at the Italian courtyard," he said, when I thought he'd already forgotten I was there. "Goodbye!" he said, and then waved, but without taking a single step away from the letters on the façade, as though he wanted to be preserved in this spot for ever, just like them.

The next day we met in the cloistered courtyard where an Afghan war veteran, playing the part of Romeo, had once jumped from the second floor without a safety rope straight into the arms of his Juliet and where, long before that, King Jan Sobieski's wife Marysieńka had taken walks. Now, neither Romeo nor Marysieńka was there, just the grey staff of the Historical Museum flitting to and fro on the balconies. Down below, at café tables, sat gentlemen with beards and ladies in high-heeled shoes who could afford cups of coffee and conversations about art. Slant-eyed waitresses went sailing by with trays, past a whitewashed statue of Themis, whose eyes might also have been slanted, although it was impossible to tell, because they'd been blindfolded once and for all – and a good thing too, or else she'd have seen the Polish students getting into the courtyard by telling the guard at the entrance that they'd come for coffee, but then just sitting under the arcades without ordering a thing, taking photos free of charge of each archway in turn, while rambling on about the battle of Vienna and ignoring the desperate holes in the Ukrainian museum's budget.

Mykola was already there, his face wreathed in tobacco smoke as he puffed on an Orbit, the brand I knew so well, and his hands took up the entire surface of the little table. I sat down beside him, but couldn't focus on the conversation – I couldn't stop obsessing about my legs, which were under the table, wrapped in the very short skirt I had put on today – it was rare for me to wear anything except jeans. The coffee that he had ordered for me was sweet and bitter, with a sort of pulp in it that I mashed with my tongue and tried to swallow.

"At home I drink instant coffee," I confessed.

"Do you like this kind?"

"Yes," I lied.

"It's called 'Fort' and it's brought here from across the Polish border. One pack costs a *hryvnia* at Halytska Square. I make myself five or six of these coffees a day."

I looked up at him and saw that instead of long hair he had sprouted Fort coffee grounds – bitter and sweet. I felt a spasm in my heart; coffee acts first and foremost on the heart, Aba would say. With a lighted cigarette in place of each of his fingers, he was shrouding the courtyard in clouds of smoke, like the kind I'd seen on television whenever Alla Pugacheva sang a sad love song. I wonder what Aba will say if I start to drink such unhealthy coffee, I thought; anyway, it doesn't matter, I'm not a minor anymore and today, to my own surprise, I've put on a miniskirt. I swallowed the last little beadlets of coffee pulp and felt my legs slip out from under me and start to climb the arcades by themselves. I've got a pretty good pair of legs, I thought in spite of myself, slender, swathed in black tights, with rays of sunlight playing on them. I wanted to catch them and quickly put them back in place, but the skirt was not an effective trap, and by now they'd taken a fancy to the top level of the courtyard and were slinking about it like cats, while I, legless and immobile, was obliged to wait for their return, before Mykola realised what was going on.

"Do you want to take a walk?" he asked, stubbing out his cigarette.

I agreed with relief. By the time we were crossing the Market Square, every part of my body had been brought under control and was running as smoothly as the Town Hall tower clock, made at Wilhelm Stiehle's German factory. We were getting close to the Boim Chapel when he said: "Call me by my first name."

I nodded, but in my very next remark, instead of a light and confident "Mykola" what emerged from me was a hiccup; I choked on the name as though it were phlegm, and it made me burp the way milk can affect a baby. I couldn't say it just like that, I felt unworthy – I needed time to get used to it. We entered a gateway, climbed some stairs, and squeezed past bits of old furniture; the rough wood made two holes in my tights – never mind, I thought, it serves them right after the tricks they played on me in the Italian courtyard. We stopped on a little balcony, where the tower of the Cathedral seemed to be too close, as if about to fall on our heads.

I was afraid that any moment now he'd kiss me, but he started to gabble as if possessed, leaning over the railing, then turning to me again, then back to the *Urbi et Orbi* pose.

"Did you know that my father was the director of the Opera? I spent my entire childhood there, I know all the shows by heart. When I was seven, there was a fire on stage during 'The Nutcracker'. The fire curtain was lowered, effectively separating the stage from the auditorium. Panic broke out, and people dashed towards the exits. But I wasn't the least bit scared. I sat there thinking it was a more interesting scene than the one before. That was the moment when I realised I wanted to be a scenographer, though I didn't yet know that word, of course. Did your mother ever tell you about the time a man in the audience died during 'Aida'?"

He showered me with dozens of memories from the Opera House like stones from a catapult, while I took root in the solid floor of the balcony – just like the audience at the ill-fated "Nutcracker", I was afraid of fire – for his words were rekindling flames of pain that I'd managed to extinguish, shattering my hard-won equilibrium, and seemed to be heralding disaster. I knew that this time I wouldn't be able to cope with it: first the Cathedral would start to burn, then the fire would spread to the houses next door to reach the balcony on which we were standing, and then it would consume the entire city – just as it had in 1527, after which the citizens had wondered if it was worth rebuilding it in the same place.

"I must go now," I cried, and ran down the stairs, hiding the holes in my tights with my hands. He came down after me without increasing his pace. He didn't reply to my words of farewell.

The Demonstration

I lay on the floor, holding her tight around the knees. Aba was holding her arms. But she wasn't looking at either of us – she was leaning out of the window, flung open wide – she'd forgotten to secure it with the latch. There was a crowd of people pouring into our little street, sinking like dough on the steps of the militia building.

"Locked them up? How many? At what time?" Mama shouted down the telephone.

It was the noise from the street that had brought me and Aba into her bedroom.

"Whatever happens, we can't let it lead to bloodshed. I'm on my way down."

Easier said than done. Her arms and legs were fettered by living shackles.

"That's an enraged crowd. They're holding stones. If they try to take the militia post by storm, that won't be the end of it. The militia will have an excuse to use force. I have to go down there."

Locked around her ankles, my fingers squeezed even tighter.

"Aaa . . . ?" Aba asked meaningfully.

"Viacheslav Maximovich is already on his way, but anything could happen before he gets here."

She started shaking her legs, in a vain attempt to break free, and asked the person on the other end of the telephone: "Are the boys who've been arrested students?"

The dark square of parquet on which my face was lying smelled of dust; someone's foot had once carved a small, crooked furrow in it that attracted me – if only I could make myself as small as Tom Thumb, and make Mama small too, take her by the hand like the Old Field Mouse with Thumbelina, and lead her through a chink underground, where there'd be a little room waiting for us, with a little table set for two, in a sweet white cottage on the banks of a stream – the same stream that Marie and the Nutcracker sailed along once he had changed into a handsome prince.

Meanwhile, she had bent down, and with a few deft movements had unhooked my fingers, without even looking at me. The overture had faded away, the flautists had gone outside for a cigarette, the double bass player had pressed his shoulders to the back of his chair, and only the violinists were on the alert, tensely waiting for the soloist's entrance, powerful as ever.

I heard the crash of the front door closing. I leaned out of the window and saw her pushing her way through to the militia post entrance, and people stepping aside to make a corridor for her, chanting her four-syllable Russian surname. She walked a little unsteadily, but only because of her stiletto heels, which were slipping on the cobblestones; she was wearing a blue dress with puffed sleeves that stood up on the shoulders. She reached the steps at the entrance to the militia post, ascended to the topmost, and made a gesture with her arms as if wanting to rise into the air. The people quietened down a little.

*"Down in the meadow the red viburnum is leaning,
There's a reason why our great Ukraine is keening,"*

She began to sing the battle hymn of the Sich riflemen in a piercing, Siren's soprano, and the crowd joined her in deep and angry voices.

*"Down in the field the golden wheat does grow,
Our Sich Riflemen are fighting the Russky foe . . ."*

I refused to believe my ears. She had said that she and Chornovil had an agreement always to leave that couplet out. Not for fear of the authorities – God forbid – but to avoid highlighting ethnic divisions that might offend anyone of Russian extraction.

"Brothers!" she cried after the final verse. "Why have we gathered in this place?"

"For our boys," said a voice from below. "We've come to free our boys ..."

"Do you agree for me to be your envoy, for me to go to the militia in your name and try to clarify whether there are any grounds at all for keeping them in custody?" she continued, and it dawned on me that any moment now she'd strain her voice – neither raw eggs nor herbal compresses would be able to save her, and it would be impossible for her to go on stage tonight; not even Maria Petrovna from the personnel department would be able to defend her; she was a fat, jolly person, who always spoke up for the female singers on the first two days of their period – yes, those days were an official reason for granting sick leave. Maria Petrovna kept an openly available calendar of the singers' monthly cycles, and if someone's time was approaching, she'd predict: "On the third of the month this girl or that girl will fall apart." What Mama had done counted as "falling apart" too, but her audience would never find out; they'd study the painted curtain through their gilded opera glasses, then start impatiently drumming their fingers on the armrests of their velvet seats, then the director of the theatre would come on stage and announce that the prima donna would not be appearing today because she was busy fighting for Ukrainian independence. Would they leap to their feet in response to this news and start to applaud? Trample their printed librettos to the floor while making a concerted dash for the exits, and come running to our windows to sing "The Red Viburnum"? Or perhaps Marianna would simply be replaced by one of the other soloists who had long been awaiting the opportunity to oust her from the theatre?

She has gone to the militia of her own volition, they'll torture and kill her, I thought, as I went to bed and tried to save myself with sleep. My dolls were very tired, all three – Alina, Arina and Aglaya. They had their own little room at the foot of my bed, with all the essential furniture: sofas, a little table and even a wardrobe, just like a real one. I made their clothes myself on an adult's Singer sewing machine, I brushed their hair and plaited it for them. Whenever they were naughty, I'd undress them, and smack their bare bottoms. When I was in a bad mood I'd wreck their entire home with my feet, tread on the furniture, the kitchenware and dresses, and then next day I would tidy it all up and they'd sit down for tea again, washed and combed, in lovely little red shoes. My dolls appeared on stage, they could sing, but more in the style of pop stars like Sofia Rotaru than opera singers like Mama.

"It's resistance through singing," said Aba to someone on the other side of the wall; the weariness was audible in her voice. "That's typical of the Ukrainian people. But what else do they have left?"

I could sleep – unlike the people below our window, who didn't disperse and go home, didn't put away their flags and didn't quieten down.

"They've been singing for two hours now!" Aba was saying to someone over the telephone when I woke up. "Marianna? I'm afraid she's still in the militia building."

She put down the receiver and went out onto the balcony. She gazed at the metal door that had closed behind her daughter; no doubt she was thinking of the Soviet saying: "There was a man, the man is gone". For a while she imagined that the people crowded into the narrow street had simply formed a queue, one of the many in this vast country of shortages, but this time it wasn't sausage, butter or polyamide tights they were waiting for, but to be taken into custody, because after all the Siberias, Kazakhstans and psychiatric prison units they'd endured, they weren't capable of dealing with what in this part of the world was called freedom anymore.

"Where's she got to now? They'll rape her, they'll torture her and wring her neck. Just remember—!" said Great-Granma, horribly loud, but then suddenly she switched to a meaningful silence. She always did that, because the words "arrest", "repression" and "1937" could never get past her lips.

"Hush now, hush," said Aba, trying to reassure her, while gently herding her off the balcony. "The child's asleep."

"Get away, you fool!" Great-Granma hissed at her. She stopped beside my bed and stared at me until I opened my eyes. In our house if anyone slept at an unusual time of day, Great-Granma would worry that they had died, and would try by all means possible to wake them – this was a habit left over from the war, when she had witnessed many deaths. I saw her face above me, with her crookedly drawn eyebrows and the long crevice of her lips. How is it possible that she is still a woman? I thought, as I watched her through my eyelashes.

All of a sudden, Mama appeared on the militia building balcony, in the company of two majors, who stood so close that their epaulettes were touching the puffed wings on her shoulders, crumpling the thin fabric. The Secession-era balustrade was too high for Aba to see Mama's hands. They must have become part of the tangle of plant-shaped railings on the balcony, which, purely because of an oversight, had never yet been straightened by the establishment's employees. Though mother and daughter shared the same eye-level, Marianna wasn't looking in Aba's direction. She called to the assembled crowd: "Friends! Brothers!"

An uneven murmur came in reply.

"Our boys are about to be released! These gentlemen here have given me their word." She paused, and then added: "But this isn't just about those of us who are here today. The main thing is that soon the walls will tumble, and the lies will end."

Applause rang out, someone plaintively began to chant "The Red Viburnum", and the sea of people undulated as the two detained students appeared at its surface, though moments later it had swallowed them up again.

"Hurrah, hurrah, hurrah!" was shouted in their honour, and the sky began to drizzle. Aba took off her wet glasses.

"Friends," cried Viacheslav Chornovil, who had finally reached the militia steps. "Time to disperse and go home."

His words were an order: the sea began to recede to the shores of the houses again, and in the dolls' room a storm erupted – the floor, beds and tables shook, the doors of the little wardrobe flew open and out fell blouses, skirts, and lastly a small bag of essential items, which every Soviet citizen had to have at home in case of dire need.

I heard Mama's voice, she was back, she was packing, leaving in a hurry for Kiev, despite the fact that there was nobody to replace her at this evening's performance – tough, she wouldn't have been able to sing today anyway.

I lay in bed, listening to her words, and also monitoring the noises that were fading away outside.

"*Down in the meadow a viburnum,*
Down in the meadow a viburnum,
Vi-burnum, vi-burnum . . ."

"Is that another song about a viburnum?"

"Solomiya Krushelnytska liked that one."

"*Vi-burnum, vi-burnum . . .*"

How beautifully she sings! Soon I was lying beside her on the floor again, as though we hadn't moved from the spot since morning.

Her slender legs were encased in the mesh of her black stockings; slightly damp with sweat, they were prickly with hairs long unshaven, and gave off a faint whiff of unwashed body – that was how her bed often smelled when she got up in the morning and went to take a shower, unaware that I would then jump into it and wrap myself in her sheets. That's so unhygienic, Aba would have said, but for me that smell contained a substance I needed in order to live. I'd try to wrest it from the crumpled fabric and keep it for myself, but it would instantly dissolve, and I'd be left alone with my mouth open and my fingers splayed.

"Don't go!"

"I must. It's very important. There are matters that nobody else can settle."

"You always have important matters to settle. I hate them."

Ignoring my words and the weight of my body on her feet, she looked through a wad of documents and packed some into a suitcase.

"*Down in the meadow . . .*"

"I promise not to get in your way. I won't say a word, as if I were deaf and dumb."

She stopped singing, and from under her naturally black eyebrows, arched like the bars of a wrought-iron Secession railing, she looked at me with a gaze I could only withstand for seconds. The words that followed landed on my head like blows:

"Where! I'm! Going! Is! No! Place! For! Children!"

I loosened my grip. Why should I hold onto her, when she was going to heaven anyway, rising enfolded in clouds like feather beds, soaring to inaccessible heights.

"Stay with me."

"Get back to your lessons this minute! Back to your dolls! I have half an hour until the taxi comes, I have to do my packing!"

With my nose in the dust, I crawled through the door. Now she wouldn't sing again until she left the house, and it was all my fault. On the tear-soaked fabric covering the sofa, a meandering map of the city streets appeared, with droshkies still driving along them, performing the same function as taxis do now, and I imagined one of them, with its hood lowered, as it carried a singer too – not Mama, but Solomiya, and not to the station, but the Opera.

Aba had just finished cooking and was sitting down in her room. From a black casket, with the profile of a man with a large aquiline nose carved on its lid, she was taking out some drawings. She never abandoned me: her legs ached, she couldn't go away.

She showed me the pen and watercolour portraits of opera singers that she had done in her youth.

"I know you had to go and study medicine," I said, "but you could have painted in your spare time, couldn't you?"

"Oh, no, no, no, my dear, certainly not during my medical studies, which I had to do in a new language that I'd only just learned! Every night I picked up a Ukrainian book and read it aloud to myself until I was hoarse."

"What about after your studies were over?"

"Have you ever heard of the job assignment system? In those days, nobody was given a job here in the city immediately after graduating. For the first few years I was sent deep into the countryside near Sambor. I did a bit of drawing there, but I needed a teacher. As I never had one, I remained an amateur."

It was out in the countryside that she discovered how much she missed Lvov. And the spreading chestnut tree that grew in the courtyard of their home – every spring it pushed its branches further forward onto their balcony, as though to offer her the helping hand of a giant and carry her away to a place she couldn't reach on her own.

When they came to live in this city in 1944, her life consisted of nothing but smells and noises, so she had to take care of the colours for herself. In her mother's room there was a piano, and in the evenings the stink of tobacco and the clanking of the keyboard drifted through the gap at the bottom of the door, as well as the clatter of army boots and ladies' heels alternating with thunderous laughter. She would close the door, wrap her head in a towel, and paint portraits of opera divas, or portraits of people she knew, including a young man with a well-defined profile.

"Your paints stink. Don't forget to shut the door when you're painting," she heard her mother say.

One morning, Great-Granma was standing in the kitchen in her dressing gown, heavily supporting her emaciated body on either side with her hands, as if to prevent its imminent fall. "Tell your suitor who spends hours loitering under our windows to go and find himself another girl!" she shouted, and then added with a sneer: "Chopin!"

Aba looked at her mother and felt her legs buckling beneath her out of almost unbearable pity – it was years since the war had ended, but her mother still bore the look of malnutrition; every time, the sight of her body made Aba feel a surge of strong emotion. "Yes, Mama, I shall do as you wish!" she said solemnly.

"Did you love that Chopin fellow?" I asked.

"Shush!" said Aba irritably, waving me aside. "What does it matter? I came back to Lvov and started working at the hospital, often doing overtime. Then I got married and had a daughter. As you know, as soon as I'd given birth, I contracted rheumatoid arthritis."

Many years later the colours started coming to the fore – once she had secured the flat in the house with the stained-glass window. She signed up for student evening courses in painting, and wasn't afraid of looking ridiculous. She'd say she was "flying" to those classes. She'd wobble, leaning on the better leg, and shoot her body forwards – she really was flying. In that period she painted most of the pictures that hung on the walls of our home.

"What do you think of this nice bouquet?" she said, showing me a sketch on the easel, as she closed the black casket full of drawings. I liked the bunch of sunflowers, but the tone in which she had asked the question was childish and hesitant. At that moment it crossed my mind that just as my dolls were would-be singers, so Aba was a make-believe painter.

Balconies

That winter in the mid-1990s, balconies started falling on people's heads, and walking close to the houses became dangerous.

"Mind your head!" went the refrain to anyone who ventured outside.

"Yesterday, on So-and-So Street, balcony mouldings from the second floor of house number six collapsed onto the head of a woman walking below," I read in the newspaper. "Although the pieces of plaster were not heavy, she was seriously injured and taken to hospital. Today, employees of the regional administration removed all projecting parts of the historic façade with the aim of preventing similar accidents in the future." I imagined Mykola's eyes narrowing with rage as he set off in search of the pieces of the desecrated façade. "No one is able to calculate how many dangerous balconies we now have in the city," declared the local council, thus legitimising further falls. Quite often the balconies fell with people standing on them, and there were also cases where balconies on their way down from a higher floor swept away the ones underneath.

The remains of the collapsed balconies were rarely removed, and the gaps that appeared in the façades were even more seldom seen to; in the city, as in our flat, there was a principle at work that any change was a sign of the will of Providence. Mykola claimed it was better this way – professional intervention carried a risk of coloured plastic sprouting on the noble grey fronts, and that was far worse than gradual, spontaneous decay.

That winter it became apparent that the city had grown weary of so many centuries of rising upwards, and was starting the process of sinking downwards, like an unstoppable landslide, crushing bumps in the terrain and dragging them after it, mixed with stones and lumps of earth. Nobody knew if the roofs might follow in the wake of the balconies, for instance, and after them whole houses, roads and people, who'd be swept away from here by the elements, heaven knows where, heaven knows at whose bidding.

That winter, it was impossible to walk quickly, the soles of the lightweight, permanently sodden, shoes that were sent to Lviv in packages from countries as mythical as Switzerland, had difficulty sliding over the dirty snowdrifts littering the streets. Old ladies ambled along with limbs fettered in plaster. They complained the least of all, because they could remember much worse times – war, famine, ethnic cleansing, and the premature deaths of their husbands. Their perfectly honed habits and a biblical hierarchy of values formed the bedrock of survival for their more fragile descendants. Indeed, in the 1990s, most of Death's victims were in their forties.

"I feel as if all my contemporaries have boarded the same train and gone, leaving me behind on the platform," Mykola told me at the time.

That winter we saw each other sporadically, always on the excuse of studying the history of some old building. After the meeting at the Italian courtyard he avoided reminiscences from the Opera – he had plainly sensed my anxiety – but it was too late; they had fallen on my poor head like a storm. It was terrifying and exhilarating, and I had no idea how to define it all. I was reliving my mother's death again, but this time my hunger for her presence was rising out of passion for her lover.

Every two or three days there was a planned power cut. Entire streets were plunged in gloom, and little flames appeared in the windows. I imagined the sound of church singing inside, and only the militia post was ablaze with secular electric light. In the darkness, Aba would switch on the radio at full blast.

"This is Kiev," it would say in Ukrainian. "The time is seven o'clock precisely."

And then came the signal for Channel One: "*Ukraina – Ukrai-i-i-na*. Today the Ukrainian Supreme Council enacted . . . "

Aba was an old lady survivalist too: she always had a bunch of fat white candles within reach, and in the corners of the flat stood candlesticks of various shapes that I would discover by groping blindly – the lack of light was no major event for her.

"The speaker of the Supreme Council of Ukraine Olexander Moroz sharply criticised the initiative of People's Movement parliamentary faction leader Viacheslav Chornovil . . ."

The blue flames in the little window of the gas boiler in the bathroom made me think of a caveman's bonfire from prehistoric times. As I undressed, my own fingers felt alien on my body: they trailed like blind men over uneven ground, drawing furrows with their tips and remembering the days when I was a three-year-old. I sat in the very same bathtub, and touched the same legs with the same fingers, sinking into a strange intoxication: Here are my legs. Here. Are. My. Legs. My. Legs. My. Legs. My. Legs.

Back then they were large, pink and warm. Nobody had asked me if I was willing for them to grow and become the downy legs of an adult woman. They had made up their own mind, ignoring me, the person on the inside – all I could do was accept the decision they had made and watch their antics from the sidelines, as I had in the Italian courtyard.

It was no different with the rest of my body – first it chose me for itself, and then it grew under my hands, becoming something completely different from Mama's body, which had been perfectly tended like a beautiful orchid in a flower pot, cut down by the precise gardener–Death. I had heard that Saint Francis of Assisi would undress his body and throw it onto thorny bushes whenever it broke free of subordination; I pinched myself on the legs, but even so my body would adamantly remain in a stubborn state of excitement – it wasn't for nothing that the saint called his "Brother Ass". I would douse myself in ice-cold water to make my body think about its behaviour – yes, it was as though I wanted to press hard on the brake pedal, but my body had chosen a different course, and it was the one in the driver's seat.

The result of my cold showers was not the one I'd planned: I fell sick with the flu, and Mykola started appearing under my windows. He'd stand downstairs with a lemon in each hand, balancing on a ripped-up paving stone, while I gestured from above, warning him to mind his head – as well as balconies, gigantic icicles were falling on people too. He disregarded my warning, staying put for such a long time that finally Aba noticed him from the next window.

"Invite him in – why is he out there in the cold? He knows the entry code."

I remember that on that particular day Great-Granma was "having hysterics", in other words lying in bed and loudly sobbing. Days like that had occurred since time began, and weren't necessarily preceded by any kind of nasty incident. "It's to do with the past," Aba would explain, and then fetch her a glass of water and a white waffle-weave towel. Meanwhile, the weeping would be intensifying, changing into whining and wailing, nothing like Great-Granma's usual voice. I imagined "the past" as uncontrolled, intermittent blubbering. For the duration of Mykola's visit, Great-Granma's "hysteria" stopped.

He entered the flat on tiptoe and waded in among the pictures. "This portrait is a complete flop in terms of composition," I heard him tell Aba. "And here you only needed to switch to a lighter colour palette . . . In that one you were dreaming of Modigliani, but in vain . . . I would only keep this watercolour."

"Yes, oh yes, yes," she chanted in delight, thirsty for the judgement of a professional. Then they had a very long chat over cups of tea, sitting outside my bedroom door, while I felt emotional: at last I had two parents, who loved each other, in the shadow of their wings I was safe, with just one condition to be fulfilled – they could talk about art, but never about music, they mustn't so much as glance at the vinyl records, or else I would develop hysteria, my tears would flow uncontrollably, forming a black lake, and then an entire sea, black as well – no God would ever be powerful enough to drain it.

"You might not have managed to recover from that blow," I heard Aba say. "The K.G.B. broke a good many people that way. But here

97

we are, you defended your doctorate, and you did that in a free, independent Ukraine. It's a pity your father didn't live to see the day."

On my way to the toilet, I saw Great-Granma at a standstill in the hall, staring at the shoes lying on the doormat, hissing away to herself, but the only words that reached me were "a man's".

I had to lie down again; I took a pill for my fever, they went on talking, and I listened in from behind the door.

"I was a boy of about six," Mykola was saying. "I ran away from my mother and went to play in the attic. I saw something unusual through a chink in the wall: there were sunbeams twinkling on some unfamiliar objects hidden behind a partition. I wasn't particularly surprised, I'd heard the fairy tales about Ali Baba and Aladdin by then, so why shouldn't I be the hero of a similar story? I called my mother, who called the lady from next door, and shortly after that they managed to get inside a previously inaccessible part of the attic. I remember their delight: they found some pictures in there, some silver tableware, and some dusty rolls of beautiful fabric. They were so taken up with all these things that they didn't notice when I furtively helped myself to a box of mysterious plates that was standing off to one side. I hid it in the attic too, but in a different spot. And later on, the day came when I fetched it out of there. It seems like only yesterday: early spring, with puddles glittering in the sunshine. I was sitting on the porch, and when I held up one of those plates, I realised it was a portrait shot of a lady in a hat. I held up another and saw an Orthodox church. Those strange plates turned out to be negatives: views of Polish Lwów and portraits of people in bizarre clothing. It was real treasure, but it was mine, hidden from sight of the adults."

"What an incredible story!" Aba said, sighing.

"Years later, I found out that before the war the villa had belonged to a Polish photographer, who went missing in the summer of 1941 and was most probably murdered by the N.K.V.D. in one of the city prisons."

"What became of the box?"

"I've still got it. And you know what, every time I hear the word 'beauty' I think of that lady in the hat, the one from the first negative. It's probably thanks to her that I became an artist."

Before leaving, Mykola dropped in to see me. He sat on the edge of my bed and ran his rough painter's hand across my brow.

"I didn't know your grandmother specialised in portraits." I could hear a slightly patronising tone in his voice, and I felt a spasm in my heart, as though I'd drunk too much Fort coffee. When he left, Aba came and took his place.

"I didn't know Mykola had a funny hat with earflaps," she said, and then added, as if betraying a secret: "After the war, the German prisoners wore those hats."

After these words she laughed brightly and girlishly, and it occurred to me that I was wronging her. Though I didn't actually know how.

Loud sobbing resounded from Great-Granma's room, gradually changing into howling, and finally singing – the piercing vocal exercise of an aged Siren. On hearing it, all sailors block their ears, turn the helm and sail as far away as possible.

Saint Florian

If someone had told me at the time that what I was going through could be described as "lust", I'd have felt slighted. As it was, I fooled myself that I was just feeling hot, and that was why I wore my coat undone as we wandered about the antiques market located near the Opera and known as "the Vernissage", where every kitschy painting, embroidered shirt or wooden spoon concealed a memory that I'd much rather not have had at all, even at the cost of all my other memories, even at the cost of my own existence. I didn't want to be there, but I let myself be led along, while Mykola did everything he could for us to keep walking past Gorgolewski's unfortunate creation, for us to cast furtive glances at it, which lingered there, hooked on the still surviving palm frond held by the figure of Glory crowning the building, or on the spot from which the statue of Lenin had been removed a few years earlier.

"What's going on at the academy?"

"I have to write an essay on an old Ukrainian commie, the poet D. I've been going to the library, I'll cobble something together eventually . . . "

"What's that?"

"You know, D. – we all had to learn his poems about the Party at junior school, and now he's become a patriot and a member of parliament. I have to write a fifteen-page essay on him for my literature class. It makes me feel sick, but I'm getting it done."

Mykola didn't respond, so I looked at him, and saw that he'd entirely constricted with anger: his forehead had concertinaed, his nose had sunk, and his eyes, brows and mouth had joined into one thin line, seeping his disapproval like saliva.

"You shouldn't make snap judgements. Nothing is ever purely black and white. Have you read his early poems? Do you know what happened to him? Did you know he was blackmailed by the K.G.B.? You haven't read them. You don't know the facts. So there."

Horrified at having enraged him so much with my stupid prattle, I fell silent. I didn't say a word until we parted, and once I was back at home I asked myself: do I really pass sentence too easily? Is it true that my judgments are hasty, perhaps even primitive? Then let him correct me, let him teach me, shape and guide me. Today he did it too severely, but never mind, there are things you have to be tough about.

I started to feel sure I had disappointed him, but the next day he called as though nothing were wrong, and suggested we meet in front of the historic fire station building. My classes went over time, and I ran to the agreed spot, but arrived very late; he wasn't there anymore.

I flattened my face against the brick wall of the fire station, and thought that this time I had more on my conscience than just stupid, ill-considered jabbering. This time I'd shown a lack of respect. How dare I make him wait for me – *he* should have to wait for *me*? A man!

A great one! A lecturer! With sorrow in his heart! People like that are addressed as sir! What am I to do now?

Without removing my face from the bricks I looked up and saw the giant figure of Saint Florian, who'd been witness to our failure to meet. At any moment I was expecting a reprimand to land on me from under his tall Roman helmet, but as befitted a martyr for his faith, Florian looked down at me kindly, and then asked: "What does Mykola really want? Isn't your body temperature rather high for a winter's day? You don't need me to aim my fireman's hose at you, do you?" Full of qualms, I rubbed my forehead against the rough surface. Mykola and I are meeting in the name of intellectual development, I replied shortly after. If it weren't for Mykola I'd never have known that you grace an alcove on the front elevation of the fire station, I wouldn't even have raised my eyes.

I looked around the scene, and saw that while waiting for me, Mykola had left sombre, adhesive glances all over it – hanging on the trees, lying on the cobbles and on the tramlines, watch out, some of them might get run over like editor-in-chief Berlioz, and I'll be to blame. I ran to the nearest phone booth to call him, but he didn't answer. Over and over again I called, then wandered the streets for ages, until finally, instead of all the monuments in the city centre I could see nothing but clusters of telephone booths, from which I tried in vain to contact him; I've called from this one, so now I'm going to try that one, and then the next one, and the one after that, but none of them contained his voice. I didn't lose heart, there were plenty of phone booths, and each one invited me inside, each one had room for me in its unlit interior, each one offered the promise of mercy and forgiveness. Finally he answered; this time the usual sorrow in his voice was a touch less sad and a touch more angry. I took off my beret, and unwound my scarf, and the meteorologically unjustified heat stirred a fleeting memory of Saint Florian. I'll make up for it, I said into the speaker, I'll come tomorrow, I'll be on time. To his studio, of course. I'm sure I'll find the gateway. I'll follow the steps down.

Glass

I'd be woken by a sudden ring at the doorbell – as its shrill sound roared in my direction like a tank, I knew it would crush me to a pulp.

I'd be woken by the murmur of Aba and Great-Granma's voices, allied as ever in the face of the common enemy; water, water, they whispered, she's poured water under our door again, she's been casting spells. Luba, the downstairs neighbour, is a wicked witch: she collects "dead water" at funerals – the water used to wash the corpse, and then spills it under our door; Great-Granma has seen her through the peephole.

I'd be woken by the whine of the front door opening, the squeal of keys hurled onto the fridge and the thud of boots falling to the floor. She'd come in on tiptoe, I'd pretend to be asleep, but the heated orbit of my bed would be waiting for her ice-cold fingers to make their fuel stop, and my nostrils would thirstily inhale the one-and-only mixture of scent, wind and tobacco. She'd leave the room, not wanting to melt in my heatwave, and go to Aba's bedroom door, while I became a radar sending her warning signals not to enter. I wonder why I felt so very scared.

I'd be woken by the murmur of the television on the other side of the door, interrupted by Aba's and Mama's verbal arias in an ever higher register – the panic would inevitably attack like a "Black Crow" van full of N.K.V.D. men.

"The Ribbentrop–Molotov pact!"

"The Nazi–Soviet military parade in Brest!"

"The annihilation of the Greek Catholic Church!"

"The millions tortured to death in the camps!"

And straight after that: "I had a right, because I was alone. You are responsible for a child."

"You were a child yourself! Fourteen years old! You stuffed hand-written leaflets about Stalin's crimes into people's letter boxes! If somebody had reported you, they'd have shot you on the spot!"

"They've already summonsed you to the K.G.B. on Dzerzhinsky Street."

"I've nothing to be afraid of."

"Marianna, you have no right to take that risk. You have a child, you have a daughter."

I'd be woken by a crash, a thump, a noise.

"Blood ties are of no significance here. I'm a Ukrainian by choice."

Had the crystal decanter fallen from the shelf, shattered and injured Mama? Had Aba dressed her wound? I would be falling asleep, and then something else would wake me up again.

In the daytime, like a dog tracking a scent, I would follow the long telephone cord that led into the bathroom. The light would be on in there, cigarettes would be burning, pine-scented shampoo would be foaming, and books would be lying spine-up on the "Siberia" washing machine. Mama would be sitting on the closed toilet seat. She'd talk to me, without interrupting her reading, just glancing up now and then from the rows of black letters. I knew her distracted air was a sham – she was like someone driving a vehicle who has to keep his eyes on the road.

"Yesterday at school we played Twenty-Seventh Communist Party Congress. One of my friends was Gorbachev, another was Yeltsin. We each had a red card for voting, like deputies."

"What issues did you have on the day's agenda?"

"We voted for the Baltic republics to leave the Soviet Union. Everyone voted unanimously in favour. Mama, will Ukraine be independent one day too?"

"I don't know, dear. We're fighting for it."

Next to the bathroom, in the narrow passage euphemistically known as the kitchen, all the burners were lit: there was water being heated for washing, soup boiling, and meat frying. Aba would leave it all, wipe her sticky hands on her apron, come to join us and sit herself down on the edge of the bath.

"I've just been reading about the brutal murder of the imperial family in 1918. Yet more proof of the fact that all our lives we've been living amid lies."

"I'll bring you more reading matter."

Mama would wash her hair, rinsing her scalp with a small saucepan; the shampoo smelled strongly of pine needles, and the odour rose off her hair in a cloud of steam. Her silk dressing gown hugged her girlish figure, and on the hip there was a patch – the residue, meticulously darned by Aba, of a piece of hot ash. There was a dressing on her hand – a memento of the nocturnal glass-breaking incident.

I would get ready for school. As I laced my shoes, I took care not to start with the left one by accident. There was a superstition: if you put on your left shoe first, your mother will die. The curbed tongue of my left plimsoll was supposed to take care of our safety.

I would go to school, and she would go to a rehearsal, a performance, less often to his studio. Years later, he tactfully disclosed to me that she didn't pamper him with visits, and told no-one at the theatre about their relationship, although they all knew about it anyway. She always appeared without warning, strode in at a rapid pace, and tossed her coat down anywhere. He wouldn't let her smoke, he'd make some coffee and say: "Sing for me!"

Her black eyebrows would cloud over, her nostrils would twitch in a predatory way, and yet he knew she was pleased. The repertoire was of no significance – it could be a folk song, a complicated aria, or some monotonous exercises. He had discovered that her voice gave her a sort of extra personality; it transformed the surrounding world, above all him – her voice was born out of her head like Athena from the head of Zeus, and the essence of that voice was abundance and excess. If nature had only granted her half as much, he thought, she'd still have been an extremely gifted singer, but nature was munificent – it despised human logic and the habit of frugality, and wanted to give more than Mykola could fit inside himself, perhaps more than Marianna could fit inside herself either, and who knows, maybe by reason of this abundance she was bound to die young, since each single note she sang was worth ten years of anyone else's life?

Yes, she rarely visited his studio, but even when she was sitting opposite him or lying in his arms, Mykola would already be missing her – even then she eluded him, and he didn't know how to define the light mist of alienation that on her initiative stood between them like a sheet of glass. They were together, and they weren't, she loved him and she didn't, if she took a step towards him, she always took two back. Before then he had heard that this is how men behave when they want to avoid obligation, but what the hell was she trying to avoid? There were only two topics that made her forget to put on the brakes – art, and the fight against the system. With rising anxiety he watched as the second began to win against the first.

One day, drained of strength, they were lying side by side on the dampened coverlet, with the record-player needle jumping in neutral gear.

"It was my faith," said Marianna. "Equality, justice, no exploitation, communism within our lifetime. I explained away the Stalinist repression – including my grandfather's death – as mistakes made by his subordinates. 'He betrayed the ideals of the great Lenin' – that's what we'd tell each other as young communists. Anyway, we didn't know the scale of the terror or the Gulag."

As he listened, he devoured her face with his eyes, and bit into the skin on her neck, breasts and belly.

"I was an idealist. My child's father and I were planning to go to the K.G.B. to ask them to issue us with guns and send us to Chile, because we wanted to fight against Pinochet. We only dropped the idea because discovering sex was more absorbing."

"Show me everything you discovered."

She freed herself from his embrace and sat up.

"All the same, in my teens I was already having moments of doubt. I remember the school assembly when everyone sang:

Lenin lives for ever, Lenin is with you now,
Lenin is here whenever you feel hope or joy or woe,
Lenin is your springtime, he's in every happy day,
In you and in me, in all of us, in every single way.

"They'd all be in ecstasy, the Russian teacher would have tears of emotion rolling down her cheeks, but I would just open and shut my mouth to cover my tracks – I was in love with a school friend, and he was my springtime, not Lenin. I would try to look around and guess who else was pretending, like me. Do you remember those assemblies?"

Mykola muttered a yes, and continued his tour of her body.

"And at the same time the atheist school was a refuge for me from Granma and her sombre, relentless devotion."

Mykola raised his lips from the freckled fields of her skin and began to croon: "*Granny and grandchild, granny and grandchild, granny and grandchild . . .*"

"So how did you cope with the communist nightmare? At school, at college, at work . . . "

"*Granny and grandchild, granny and grandchild . . .*"

Lithe as a whippet, he shifted his body to the grand piano, and started to play a jazz standard.

"As you're ignoring my question, I'll answer it myself. You knew the truth from your mother, but you had to keep your mouth shut. You learned your own family history from meaningful silences, furtive glances, half smiles and oblique remarks. Later on you read samizdat and listened to the 'enemy' radio."

"My refuge from the regime was the Polish People's Theatre."

"I used to think the sort of people who belonged to national organisations were rather limited, but perhaps I'll change my mind."

"The plays of Różewicz and Mrożek were like a window onto another world. There aren't just Poles at the Polish theatre, you know. Our director, Valery Bortiakov, is Russian, but he's thought up an alternative way of defining his ethnicity – he says he's a Lvovian. I feel the same way too, although I'm a native Ukrainian."

"Polish culture as a window onto Europe . . . So did you fall through that window eventually?"

Mykola smiled wryly.

"No, I was just thrown out of college. Talking of the fight – my mother saw you at a rally. And she told me she'd rather hear you in the public square than at the theatre."

"I never thought I'd end up singing in the streets. But as you know . . . 'art belongs to the people', doesn't it?"

"They've already summonsed you to Dzerzhinsky Street."

"But you know what? I'm not at all scared. The other day some workers brought me a bunch of roses that pricked my fingers badly. And it occurred to me that the first blood in the fight against the regime had been shed."

After these words, Marianna started getting dressed; Mykola stood up from the piano, lay down at her feet and immobilised her knees.

"Please stay the night, I beg you!"

"I've got a rehearsal tomorrow morning, and a show in the evening. And there's a political meeting in between."

"As you wish," he replied meekly, drawing the curtains across the rapidly blackening windows.

The Studio 1

It was dark by now; clad until recently in uneven cobblestones, now the street that led to my destination was rearing under me, as I tried to curb it with my booted feet, but instead I fell into a hole, down to the level from a hundred years ago. I'd always longed to travel to Lwów, the city of the past, never the future, but I soon realised this wasn't a time machine, just road repairs – they'd removed some of the old cobbles but not yet laid the new ones, and in the meantime the working day had ended, the workmen had gone home to their villages and forgotten to put up a warning sign saying "Beware, roadworks", not that anyone in Lviv would expect such a courtesy from them anyway. Stuck briefly in a sort of idealised in-between world, I gazed at the surrounding trees and villas from a level close to the collapse of the Austro-Hungarian Empire and the Polish–Ukrainian war, as the unsung notes quivered in my throat – I couldn't be late for this meeting.

I stepped out of the pit, but even so, from here the street ran downhill beneath my feet, lower and lower and lower; his house was at the very end. I went through the gateway, down some steps, opened a door, then a second one, and a third, too young and self-absorbed to remember to close them behind me, then he opened the last one to greet me, and at once I knew he wasn't angry with me anymore for yesterday's lack of punctuality.

He invited me inside, and I entered a room where the laws of gravity didn't apply – there were 3-D models hanging on the walls, a man's death mask on the ceiling, and in between them swayed a grand piano, surrounded by bookshelves and vinyl records, and an easel too, with an unfinished sketch of someone's wrinkled fingers. We chatted about this and that, until finally my gaze fell on a piece of drawing paper lying on the table, and I asked what the geometric shapes on it meant.

He sat down in the circle of light cast by a small lamp; his earring flashed, and so did the wedding ring on his finger, as he showed me to an armchair opposite. He laid a new sheet of paper on the desk, drew a few small circles in one corner, then triangles in another, and a thick line to separate them.

"On the right is the land of circles. Circles marry circles, and then produce circular children. On the left the triangles reign. Here only triangles marry triangles, and together they have little triangles. This line is the border, and the area around it is the borderland, where other children are born."

He drew circles inside triangles and squares inside circles, and also – these I liked the most – some polygonal shapes made of overlapping circles and squares.

"People would love these children to define themselves as one shape or the other. But the catch is, they refuse to. They're one and the other all at once, and that's what makes them unique. But most people won't accept that sort of choice – hybrid or mixed shapes.

Most of them want unambiguous definitions. It's easier to live that way."

"What about you?" I asked.

"I'm a cross-breed of this very kind. A borderland person."

So am I! I wanted to cry out, but I lacked the courage. By now I knew I had to be careful about making public declarations. After a pause, I said in an enquiring tone: "Aaaa?"

The vowel vibrating in my throat changed into syllabic singing, then vocalese and mormorando.

"Mama used to visit you here at the studio . . . " I said, wanting to ask a question, but it came out as a statement, which I instantly regretted; his brows and forehead knitted in the familiar way, which caused the rest of my unasked questions to stick in my throat along with the unsung notes.

I was sitting next to a hot tile stove, and on the other side of my chair there was a bookcase. Mykola stood over me, and started removing art books from the shelves. He was so proud of each one that I dared not ask if I could borrow them one day; he didn't put any of them back in their place but kept handing them to me. I sank into the armchair, more and more oppressed by albums, my knees encumbered by the grand weight of them, holding a heavy tome in each hand, and resting my feet in their thick woollen socks on others. My head was level with a shelf filled with another dozen he hadn't yet removed, but I was already having just as tough a time as the Atlases and Atlas-esses, I meant to say the caryatids, who held up the city's balconies; here I was, wielding the Northern Renaissance and Baroque woodcarving, while clothing myself in the Secession, and stepping on Hutsul embroidery. I was revelling in the cluster of gems he was adorning me with, but at the same time the enforced immobility was troubling me. The lack of an emergency exit was contrary to all the rules of safety, and I would have liked to stand up. Then I discovered I was pinioned – his finger was fluttering near my temple, twisting a ribbon of my hair around it. I was pinioned – his brass head was rolling onto my knees, pushing its way through the heaps of books. I was pinioned, as his voice uttered a simple phrase more suited to the gentlemen of old, playing the social flirt: "I find you very pleasing."

As I observed the once organised, now collapsing structure of my notions about the world, his words were like a road crash; I knew these things happened to others, but to be a participant, who knows, maybe even the perpetrator – who could say if we'd be able to get out of it in one piece?

"What are we going to do about this?" I could hear the pitiful words pressing at my lips as I thought that now he would have to remove his clever head from my knees and instantly place it under the speeding train that from this minute was carrying the two of us towards each other, but he nimbly freed me from under the pile of books, set me on my feet, leaned me back against the hot stove and began to kiss me on the mouth. He's got a red sweater, I thought, returning his kiss, Saint Florian was absolutely right.

The cold air eased the effects of our arousal as, weak from kissing, we wobbled our way along tree-lined Tolstoy Street, our boots sliding across the bumpy surface.

"What are we going to do about this?" I finally asked. I lacked the words to explain to him how terrifying it was to feel my lust slipping out of my control – it was just as frightening as the feeling that my memories of the Opera had been changing lately because of him; meanwhile my intuition was telling me to beware of people who have the power to change your memories. Is that what I'll tell my daughter one day, beware of the man who knows more about you than you know about yourself?

Instead of answering, he led me into a gateway and made a speech about its sculpted ceiling, adorned with stucco topped up with marble dust, while I thought about the ugly bulges in it, and the hideous coloured decorations on the festive garlands of spruce surrounding it. We kissed underneath them too.

"Please don't call me ever again," I said. It was probably my last chance to get out of the love triangle with my dead mother in the background.

"As you wish," he replied.

I already knew our words couldn't change much.

Cathedral

The Lord God would appear to me after the lights went out. I could play in the dark with my dolls, who had their own room at my bedside. I could hum songs to myself. I could shamefully touch certain parts of my body. Or feel sad for no reason, follow the shadows of cars as they crossed the ceiling, or unintentionally eavesdrop on the adults' conversations through the wall. I knew it was God the Father who visited me, far more credible than the impassioned Jesus, streaming with blood. Somebody had told me that He was called the Almighty.

Whenever God came down from the bookcase, I fell to my knees before Him. I'd be trembling with fear that one of the household would see me like that. On one unique occasion, God called on me in the bathroom, just as Aba was coming in. She didn't say a word when she saw me kneeling there, but just smiled enigmatically.

God, like Poland, belonged to a world that had been cancelled long before I was born. I started looking for information about Him. In Great-Granma's room I came upon a prayer book, so I took it away and hid it in my desk drawer. Its yellowing pages were mostly full of rhymes in unfamiliar, pre-war spelling: "Angel of God, my

Faith is in Thee, Ever stand on Guard by me", "Thou art the Way, the Truth and the Light, Lord of Mercy and of Might", "Lord, forgive my Sinful Ways, Love and Guide me all my days". How idiotic, I thought, maybe because from the moment of my conception I had been nurtured on exquisite poetry. If I were to write a summary of this handbook on How to Sigh Soulfully, it would go more or less like this: Man spoke to God, but God refused to listen. Man did not lose heart, but went on talking. Man wanted a lot of things from God, but God was in two minds about giving him anything. Man had done something wrong in the past. God knew about it, and Man knew that God knew. Nevertheless, Man was very keen for God to give him a second chance. I was surprised Man was so servile towards God.

It occurred to me that God should be legitimised in some way.

"Have me baptised!" I told Aba.

"I've done it already!" she replied.

Then it came to light that in my infancy Aba and Great-Granma had organised a baptism for me at home. An old priest from the Polish Catholic Cathedral had insisted on my mother's consent, but a note in the yellowed prayer book stated that in certain situations anyone can perform a baptism without anybody else's approval. One day, when Mama had gone to college, those two not very saintly women, those high priestesses without ritual robes or the blessing of the church authorities, drew the curtains in the main room and doused me in holy water stolen from the Cathedral, believing that this makeshift act would cleanse me of the stigma of original sin.

"Is that baptism valid?" I asked doubtfully. There was no reply.

The "Latin Cathedral" was located at the centre of the city – the stone inside the peach. Locked and bolted, this mighty edifice didn't look like a place for children, but I had once managed to get inside. God was a lack of electrical power, I'd been told at school, but the Cathedral was nothing but light, in the form of lots of gleaming grapevines – they shone gold, sparkled, shimmied down from the cupola to the floor and then twined their way back up again. In their brightness, a lady in black was kneeling. Her head and shoulders were covered by a scarf, and the tail of a rosary trailed behind her. She rocked from side to side, then lay down and began to wriggle across the floor. Religion is the opium of the people, I thought, as I gazed at her.

When Aba and I walked up to the closed black door, first we had to knock with our keys, which broke their heads and teeth as they rapped against the metal. After a while a very pale woman with a boyish haircut appeared on the threshold. We followed her across a dark vestibule chaotically stacked with furniture, inhaling the scent of lilies and cellars, as I dragged the Lord God from my room at night after me on a lead. We went up and down steps that were awkward for our little feet – size thirty-five and a half; behind one of the doors we passed, a light was burning and someone was playing the piano. We slid across the slippery floor as though on skates, until we were cast up right by the altar. A limping man in a white robe was blowing out the candles that stood on it, while a cat with protruding ribs wound around his legs. From the unlit altar, the stems of tall stained-glass windows rose to the heavens, while sunbeams shining through them changed into many hues and cast their light on the very pale woman, flickering in her static pupils. We passed long dead knights in armour slumbering in side naves – an old woman was rubbing her entire body against them, whispering to herself; she looked like Great-Granma.

The small side altars were crowded with vases of red and white peonies, while young girls kneeled beside them, tearing off the petals and putting them into little cloth bags. I looked up: where arches like the ribs of the cat at the feet of the man in the white robe joined to form a Gothic vault, I could see a gap, and a patch of blue sky showing through it – the Cathedral was full of holes! Today it's sunny, I thought, but what about other days? Does the rain pour and the hail shower on the heads of the congregation? They've been through worse things in life, I answered myself, this minor nuisance wouldn't make much of an impression on them. And as I was standing there with my face turned upwards, I noticed a miniature lady in a crown looking at me from on high, rising above the altar like the sun, surrounded by a rainbow. Aba had disappeared.

A nun came up to me in a stiff, black-and-white robe, her small, grey eyes peeping out from under it. She took my hands in hers, and started guiding them up and down, while she repeated: in the name of the Father and the Son. I remembered that Great-Granma said the same thing every night, but then the nun painfully rapped me on the fingers, which weren't showing the required dexterity. She led me to a closed side chapel, handed me a little yellow book entitled *Come, my Jesus*, and said I was to learn it by heart. There were stained-glass windows in the chapel too, featuring a sad, grey man leading a donkey with the Virgin Mary on its back. I would have liked to sit astride a donkey like that too, and let myself be led to some other, better land, to a fortified town that would give me shelter and where I could stay for ever.

The makeshift baptism was recognised, so now I had to prepare for my first holy communion, Aba declared when we met near the exit. The woman who'd been praying beside the relief sculpture of a knight went past us in the vestibule. She plunged her velour sleeves into a strange alcove, and a few drops of water fell to the floor. I was almost certain it was Great-Granma. The dour nun saw us to the door.

"*Do widzenia!* – Goodbye!" I said to her in farewell, proud of my Polish.

"You can't speak like that in church!" she snapped in reply. "That's what you say in the street outside. This is the House of God, in here you must say: '*Niech będzie pochwalony Jezus Chrystus!*' – Jesus Christ be praised!"

"*Niech będzie pochwalony Jezus Chrystus!*" I repeated, and the black door crashed shut behind me.

Since time began, whenever Great-Granma was having a good day, she drew the curtains, sat at the mirror with a pair of tongs and curled her hair, while singing a song with a chorus that sounded like the noise of a cuckoo. Sometimes, she wailed strange, repetitive lyrics, such as: "The righteous man dwells on thy holy mountain. The ri-i-i-ghteous man dwells on thy holy mountain."

Whenever I heard her shrill voice, I felt embarrassed, just as I did when she pissed in my presence – I thought of that voice as a form of indecent exposure.

When I started going to Mass at the Cathedral, I realised that the strange lyrics were psalms. There were also occasions when I encountered Great-Granma in the vestibule, standing by the stoup and liberally dousing her nose and chest with water from it.

"Yes, from time to time she sings in the Cathedral choir," Aba confirmed, gazing off to one side. Could it be that she regarded the singing as a form of indecency too?

"Did she and Great-Grandfather meet in the choir?"

"In 1925, Great-Granma was one of the first women to be accepted into the Leningrad State Capella Choir, and despite being very young, she was soon the deputy conductor. Yes, she and your great-grandfather really did meet at a rehearsal – he was one of the tenors."

I stared out of the window at the red bricks of the house next door, laid bare in a spot where the plaster had crumbled off the façade. I had often been told that in the sunlight the bricks were the colour of my great-grandfather's hair. His face loomed easily out of the pattern of cracks, and I imagined him singing from dawn to early winter dusk: while it grew dark outside the windows and the other choristers said goodbye and went off home across the bridges of St Petersburg, a celebratory duet continued to resound in the rehearsal room, for there they remained, she the conductor and he the singer, she the mezzo-soprano and he the tenor, a slip of a girl and an adult male, a small woman and a tall man singing non-stop for several days on end, a whole month perhaps. This was their vocal marathon, just like my parents' poetic version.

"Papa was ten years older than Mama," Aba said. "And he came from a better family – they had a landed estate in Lithuania, which they lost, of course, but Mama's parents were peasants from the same region who had come to St Petersburg in search of a living. Papa's family was opposed to the marriage! Even many years later, when his sister was an old woman, she refused to meet me. But Papa was very much in love anyway, and wouldn't listen. They got married at the

Catholic Church of Saint Catherine, without any witnesses. But you know that, don't you?"

I nodded. I imagined it was cold in the rehearsal room; the janitor who tended the stove had gone home by now, and yet the male singer had sweat on his brow, the closeness of the female conductor was warming him with her smooth, white skin, her dainty hands and feet (we'd all inherited them from her), and by the strength of his love Great-Grandfather caused the polar night to fall in Leningrad for thirty days on end, he refused to let anyone disturb their intimacy – neither his domineering sister, nor the irascible empress Catherine the Great, in honour of whom this church was built, nor the wretched Stanisław August Poniatowski, her former lover and last king of Poland, who was buried in it for a time, nor the singers in no need of a conductor, who right now were in the far North, building kilometres of barbed-wire fences, as long as the notes of the two songbirds' loudest allegro.

"They were together for seven years. In 1937, Papa sensed the danger of the situation, but he wasn't daunted. He was impetuous by nature, and went around saying what he thought, but in those days there were informers at every step. People started to vanish from the flats in our house: usually men, but women too – my neighbours, twin girls, lost their mother and father at one stroke. I wasn't asleep when they came for Papa. He kissed me goodbye, and said it was an error, he'd be back soon, while two men stood waiting for him in the doorway. I never saw him again."

Her father's arrest had become the focal point in Aba's life; sooner or later every story she told ran aground on it like a ship on a sandbank.

"I know, I know, I've heard it all before. Tell me about the singing!"

In reply she did something to her face – she put out the light in her eyes, clenched her lips, and held her hands to her ears; just her nostrils went on quivering like the wings of a bird.

"After that the singing stopped for ever," she said.

Somehow I knew she wasn't telling the truth.

Paintbrushes

Mykola liked to spread my paintings on the floor, and then walk among them barefoot, pointing his toes at the successful bits, though the shocking majority of them were useless. Every time, we lay on my bed afterwards, I thought about the coloured stains on his feet and in breaks between kisses, he continued his disquisition on why I was a bad painter. Hearing Aba's footsteps approaching the door, we'd sit up, and Mykola would put his feet back on the painted sheets of paperboard.

"This line of reasoning is highly familiar," he'd loudly say. "You think you're the first to do it, but you're following a well-trodden path."

"At the drawing stage, the shapes are inspired by Far-Eastern art," he'd carry on. "But that's not the main problem. There's a lack of dominant themes. Tell me what this picture is about."

"You're wrong!" I'd interrupt him heatedly. "There is a theme, there is a dominant theme, there is a meaning! It's about a tree. About its roots and branches. And about the light, that's . . . that's . . . playing on them."

In the course of these debates I'd soon begin to splutter and lose my voice – as if the connection were weakening between my chest, where my arguments were born, and my speech organs.

"Let's leave the content aside – let's talk about the emotions. You've got far too many of them. You keep introducing trembling, twinkling, tearfulness – what a bland, feminine daub."

Worst of all, he was reading those comments off my heart, where they'd been lying hidden from the start – underneath my lungs and diaphragm, deep in the pit of my stomach.

"And yet it's not the emotions, not even the mixture of conventions that is your greatest mistake – this could be fixed. Nor is it the lack of a dominant theme – after all, you could create one. The problem is that what you're doing is derivative. You're not speaking with your own voice."

I liked it when he criticised me – it made me feel as if what I was doing mattered.

"You're studying," Aba would reverently state when she put her head round the door. "I've made you some sandwiches."

We'd go to his place, and on the way I'd tell him how I had started to paint. One day, Aba had taken me to the *hudozhka*.

The art school, otherwise known as the *hudozhka*, was situated behind the Mickiewicz monument: the poet is receiving a lyre from the hands of a winged muse, and it's all happening at the foot of a splendid column, the top of which is crowned by nothing other than a paintbrush! Similar, smaller paintbrushes decorated the roof of the house next door, home to the "Friendship" international bookshop, where Aba used to buy Polish magazines – "Cross-Section", "Woman and Life", or "Beauty". Mickiewicz was turned to face what Aba called "the beautiful shop". Officially it was called "Hudozhnik", "the

Artist", and it sold pictures, paints and hand-made jewellery. Just as in the grocery stores of the time, the lighting inside was weak, and right at the entrance, semi-darkness greeted us. On the walls hung views of the city, landscapes and still lifes; there was a small white card attached to each picture with a three-figure number and the artist's name written in unfamiliar letters in the bottom corner. Aba always said you shouldn't look at paintings from close range – you had to step back a dozen paces to be able to take the whole thing in visually, but here, in two small showrooms, that was difficult to do – there were canvases covering every square centimetre of the walls, and standing on the floor too, so whenever I attempted to achieve the crucial distance, I would just see one enormous picture: it was a landscape and a cityscape, a portrait and a still life all at once; I wondered if Mickiewicz had a better vantage point from his column.

The sales ladies at the Artist wore dark, embroidered folk shirts and several strings of burgundy-coloured beads, which began at their necks and ended below the glass covering the long counters they stood behind; like the pictures, the beads had tags attached with three-figure numbers. The ladies spoke a completely different Ukrainian than the shop assistants at the grocery stores – these ones uttered grand words, as if they weighed as heavily on their throats as the beads did on their necks, as if every word had a tag with a three-figure number attached to it too. I knew we couldn't afford to buy anything in here, but every time Aba played the same game with them: she'd ask about the prices of the canvases, examine the jewellery and the cutglass vases, and jostle the paints and brushes. The ladies would answer slowly, without emerging from behind the counters, and I'd wonder whether they ever went home at all – perhaps they were locked in here for the night, put away in special cases like cellos.

The art school was located in a large residential building; at the time nobody knew that a few years later it would fall into ruin, and everything would be evacuated from it, including the shabby cinema on the ground floor, which would mean it could be quite officially demolished. Soon it would be joined by the Soviet Union, and they'd fall apart in parallel, in a race – nothing could save them from a hideous death right at the heart of the city, though the building would outlive the empire. Just before its demise, the young people would cover it in colourful slogans; later on, the city would miss it, like somebody missing a front tooth, except that no-one would know if the gap it had left was a sad, senile one, or a temporary one between milk and permanent teeth.

When I first went to the art school to start my classes, none of this was of any significance. I learned to set up a heavy wooden easel, tacked my first piece of paperboard to it with drawing pins and made my first line on its smooth surface without any hesitation.

The shapes of the sculpting tools, each of them concave at one point and convex at another, the plasticine rain outside the windows, our benches set around a bath full of clay – there we sat in grey, long-sleeved overalls. The tutor, who had enrolled me at the art school, must have lost a finger in the war; it was the war that he'd mutter about as he walked along the corridors, laughing into his black beard. That day he had given us a task – each of us was to sculpt a human head, we were to model for one another – and then he had left the room. Working in silence, now and then we reached into the bath, as each of us kneaded his football; my model was Nina, and the rest of the group were boys. A murmur gradually rose in the classroom, and after a while the pack of boys abandoned their work and surrounded the two of us in a tight circle.

"Whack, whack, don't hold back!" one of them began. The rest responded in chorus: "Bust and dust up the Russkies!"

They kept bellowing this little ditty, while jumping around me and Nina, and waving their sculpting tools about. It was a game, not a fight – close up I could see their clownish faces, their big tongues and their dancing fingers. But the next moment it turned out they weren't going to release us from the circle – we were in a trap. On and on they chanted: "Russkies out! Russkies out! Russkies out!"

The first wet clod hit me on the head, followed by the next, and Nina got hers in the face. The boys were soon rid of the lumps of clay destined to be heads, leaving them with nothing – now we girls had access to the bath. The classroom smelled like a botanical garden in early spring as I scooped the stuff up by the handful, moulded cannonballs out of it and battered our opponents' heads with them. I managed to breach the blockade at the level of the smallest boy, whose name was Tsitovich, the leader of the pack, and now, although I could have escaped, I put my arms around his waist and jammed a wad of clay into his hair. Tsitovich is alive, the thought crossed my mind, as I alternately touched his warm head and the cold clay.

"I didn't know I was a Russky."

Nina and I were sitting in the locked toilet; she cast me a suspicious look.

"It's them, they've got horns!"

"What's that?"

"They've got horns – they're *raguls*, to put it another way."

"What are *raguls*?"

"*Ragul* is a local word for an ethnic Ukrainian, and literally it means 'horned'. My mother says: 'I won't let you leave the house if you're going out with a *ragul!*'"

The teacher laughed to himself, hid his face in his crippled hands, and in his company we went back to the classroom, which was buzzing with activity, as if nothing had happened. A row of clay heads of various sizes stood on the edge of the bath, gaping at us.

My umbrella leaked and my shoes were soaking wet, despite which I trailed along the streets, floundering on pavements that under the pressure of mud and water appeared to have lost their hardness. Nina's thinking about her *ragul* boyfriend now, I said to myself, she's even discussing it with her mother – she's going to share her umbrella with a tall young man instead of me, they'll go out for ice cream together, they'll go to the cinema and back to her house, and when her mother opens the door, her hackles will rise – for sticking out of his hair he'll have the twisted horns of a bull, a pair of branching antlers, or the slender white spike of a unicorn.

Great-Granma called them "the locals". A word is a word, but she would say it in a special way, making it cut like a blade. "Local" came from the Latin word *locus*, meaning place – my place was Lviv, so I'd say, "I am a local too", and in reply she'd laugh spitefully, just as Nina had laughed at me in the art school toilet.

The art class incidents revealed to me that each person has an ethnicity. Before then I had thought ethnicity only concerned those who were especially interested – Aba, for example, who was always talking about her Polish identity. As for others, at our first lesson in the first year at school we'd had to learn the Soviet anthem by heart, including the verse about "Russia, who has united within her" all the nationalities of the fifteen Union republics. At the time, I imagined her hiding them in her great belly, and that they felt warm and comfortable in there. There was one ethnic group that was never mentioned among the "united" nations – Aba and Great-Granma always paused after uttering this name – *the Jews*. Only one other name was characterised by a similar degree of anxiety – *the Lord God*. Aba uttered the former with as much apprehension as reproach. The latter she drew into her lungs with the air: *the Looord*, and then she let it drop with a thud: *Goddd*. It sounded as though she were casting an accusation at the Jews, while God in turn were casting one at her.

"I am a Pole, to the marrow of my bones," she used to say.

"I am a Ukrainian, by choice," said Mama.

"Russkies out!" the boys shouted at me.

"I am of Lvovian ethnicity," Mykola repeated after his guru, Valery Bortiakov. This last approach suited me best.

Mickiewicz couldn't be seen from the windows of the art school, just the airborne naked legs of his muse, flying up to him on his small island amid the sea of cars. Once I asked Aba why the Poles hadn't taken him away to Poland too, since they had carried off Fredro the playwright and King Jan Sobieski; at the time she had explained to me that he was very firmly incorporated into the city centre, so they'd have had to take the entire square along with him, and all the houses standing around it. That's a weighty argument, I conceded with relief – Mickiewicz had been saved, the man and his long green hair, the man and his many-stringed lyre, the man and his bare-legged muse, about which I wasn't sure – was it a boy or a girl? Heaven knows, perhaps now one, now the other, or maybe both at once; the body was covered with an airy robe, and I wondered if on frosty nights the poet removed his overcoat and wrapped the muse in it. I also wondered if the column had ever been crowned with a sharpened pencil, rather than a brush – I had heard that, in days of yore, Mickiewicz was nicknamed "The Pencil".

"It took a pretty long time for the pre-war citizens of Lwów to be persuaded by this monument," Mykola said.

We'd walk from the Opera to Mickiewicz, and turn a circle around him, examining the way he was designed to fit the profiles of the various buildings. One day, we perched on the island, surrounded by a sea of cars, and he told me about something that had happened in the early 1980s. I'd been waiting for this for ages, but Mykola rarely shared important stories from his life with me – he was like a collector whose fear for the safety of his exhibits is greater than the pleasure he derives from looking at them.

"I remember that in those days, the Mickiewicz column was like a guard tower, one of millions in this land of gulags. The actors at the Polish Theatre surrounded the monument in a tight circle on the pedestal steps, and the narks were standing a little further off, on the pavement. True to tradition, we'd come with flowers – we did that every year at the start of the theatrical season. I remember that on that occasion we'd brought gladioli with red-and-white ribbons. We could feel in the air that something bad was going to happen – the news about Solidarity had come through from Poland, Poland was starting to have very bad associations for *them*, and we were performing at the Polish People's Theatre. We laid the flowers, and then *they* came up and checked the identity cards of everybody present. The next day we all lost our jobs or were thrown out of college. People of six ethnicities, for Polish bourgeois nationalism."

"What happened to you?" I asked.

"I was removed from the list of students at the Lviv Academy of Fine Arts, which wasn't called that yet."

In old age, Mykola's father mellowed – if he'd had a son of school age now, he wouldn't have made him spend all his afternoons in a stuffy house. From his post as director of the Opera, he passed into retirement, and developed an interest in woodwork – he'd knock together clumsy little tables and stools, littering the conjugal bedroom with shavings. With age, his devotion to the Soviet system grew weaker; for its sake he had fought on the front lines in the Great Patriotic War, after which he had moved from Kharkov to Lvov. First, the years he spent in a managerial job had taught him that within this system hypocrisy, cronyism and bureaucracy are insurmountable, and then he'd been affected by many years of living with his wife, who could count more than one member of the Ukrainian Insurgent Army among her relatives. The further Mykola's father distanced himself from the lofty ideals whose implementation prompted horror and disgust, the more his once glaring gaze began to fade, and even to take on a new, feminine look.

Something different had happened to Mykola's mother. The more her formerly tyrannical husband mellowed, the more sharply she began to express herself; the less he counted away from home, the more confidently she came outside – above all to the meetings held by various pro-Ukrainian circles, and later to demonstrations. It was Blitzkrieg on a grand scale, and only her female friends were surprised by her rapidly progressing obesity, though it didn't seem to bother her because, for her, the broadening of her body was on a par with the acquisition of unknown territories, and the rising feeling that this house and this city belonged to her.

At the news that Mykola had been sacked for Polish nationalism, his mother went pale, seized her temples and instantly realised that his father must never know at any cost. So they made an agreement that for the next few months, Mykola would leave the house as usual, pretending he was still attending classes. At the same time, she initiated her husband into a secret plan to reclaim the rooms in the basement, which had recently been vacated on the death of the tenant, a pre-war dipsomaniac. His father had willingly joined in with this task, renewed his contacts at the city council, arranged the formalities and reacquired the space, which was ideally suited for practising his new hobby. But he made use of it only briefly – he died of a heart attack a year after the events below Mickiewicz's column, just as Mykola was taking his first steps at the new college that had accepted him.

His father's death meant that all Mykola's former successes, his first-class diploma from the Kharkov Academy of Fine Arts, his work as a set designer at the Opera, and even his PhD from his Lvovian alma mater, had a bitter aftertaste. Marianna's voice had freed him from a sense of undoubtedly imaginary guilt. It transported him beyond his own and his family's history, into a sphere where there is heaviness and lightness, and many of the other, often contradictory things that comprise personal freedom.

It was the same thing, I think, that he sought in me – that was why he began our awkward, nonsensical affair. Nothing good would come of it; as I stressed at the start, I was entirely devoid of musical talent.

Lenin

"I'd rather not take you with me, because it's not a place for children. But since you insist – after all, you are fourteen already," said Aba.

Back then, I was giving the Opera a wide berth, but this day was going to be exceptional, the show was due to take place outside, and spectators were closing in from all directions. It was September 1990. By now, Mykola had his set designer's degree, and had been working at the Opera for several years. That day, we were both in the crowd, as yet unaware of each other's existence, but both thinking about Marianna. To Mykola, the whole event contained too much politics and not enough art, so he was feeling overwhelmed by a melancholy yearning for her voice – it isn't there, he thought, neither in heaven nor on earth, and he wondered how that "isn't" differed from his own "is", and whether or not his own "is" – or rather "am" – had atrophied more since Marianna's death than it had before he met her. For me it was the total opposite – her words came back to me: We are humus, we give up our lives to fertilise the soil, we shall never see its harvest. I imagined I was taking part in an opera that had come out in front of the theatre and was being performed for everyone – "Art belongs to the people" – and Mama's voice was taking the lead in it.

I looked up: crowning the tympanum as ever was the allegory of Glory with her palm leaf, tired of the fact that the shows were always held inside the building – perhaps it was she who had called this gathering together. The golden frond in her hands was sending out sparkling rays in the sunlight, but the real star of today's programme was situated closer to the ground, and I was the only one not looking in his direction. I stepped onto the edge of a bed of daisies, with my chin touching the crown of Aba's head: there was a city on the golden map of her hair, with the white threads of highways running off in various directions before disappearing in a tangle of darker local roads. Angry faces surrounded us, at first in a single circle, later a double and treble one; I could tell that very soon it would be impossible to get out of there. Nervously I did up the row of buttons on the trendy denim jacket that I'd inherited from Mama; it still smelled of tobacco and grown-up scent, and at one point a button was missing, so there was a safety pin instead.

There I stood, with my gaze fixed on Glory, nodding her head as the choir came in – today's performance would be without an overture. The choir sang in two parts: the altos wailed against the desecration of the leader, while the bassos demanded his overthrow. Between them stood cadets from the officer's training school, in silence, not yet knowing if their part would be included in the general score. I remember that the altos – the opponents of the overthrow, in other words – were jittery and tearful, as though wrapped in crunchy sheets of foil like the stiff little heads of red carnations, whereas the bassos – the supporters – were old, work-worn and robust; the black-eyed saints from the church banners had come out on their side. Among the altos were the lady teachers from my school. Why were they defending him, I wondered in surprise? What did they need him for? Hadn't they read about the Red Terror? Hadn't their fathers been shot? Weren't their grandfathers sent to Siberia? We are humus, we give up our lives to fertilise the soil, we shall never see its harvest, as Mama said. But what about those women, trying to fertilise it with their tears?

"Hands off Lenin!" they wailed.

"Suitcase – station – Russia!" the others snarled back at them.

"Let's hope they remove his corpse from the mausoleum and bury it at last," said Aba. "Then he'll stop radiating his evil power and addling people's wits."

"Mother Mary, our Intercessor, let it not come to bloodshed," a lady said next to us, sighing.

"Out! Out! Out!" cried the two choirs, merging into one.

She's just about to start, I thought, and already I seemed to hear the solo: We are humus. We shall never see . . .

"*Forte!*"

I looked up again: her hands were fixed in a gesture that sent the orchestra one more signal, and suddenly I heard a clatter: the golden palm frond had fallen onto the heads of those taking part in the performance – Glory had finally let go of it.

"*Forte! Forte! Fortissimo!*"

All at once the musical scores became confused in the choristers' hands and flew to the ground, the voices began to sing out of tune, I heard a howl, a rasp, and a moan, I was pushed away from Aba, I crouched on the ground and folded my hands across my chest, I clasped them, and then locked them together behind my back, sand and dog-ends fell on my head; meanwhile, standing on tiptoe, the Mother-Mary-our-Intercessor lady reported: "They're setting the banners aside. They're tearing the carnations from those people's hands. They're whipping them across the face with them. Now that lot are spitting on the blue-and-yellow flags. And the soldiers are driving them apart."

My legs ached from squatting down, and I sank to the paving stones; luckily Aba had disappeared, or she'd have started bleating about letting my ovaries catch cold. Down on the ground, I discovered that Mrs Intercessor had men's orthopaedic boots, one bigger than the other – she must have had polio in childhood. There were long laces joining not just the tops of her boots, but also her legs – she was like a hobbled horse, and I wondered how she had got here; then it occurred to me that maybe all of us present had our legs tangled in her laces, and if any one of us made a move, thousands of others would be dragged after. You must never sit down in a crowd – they'll trample you to death. Aba had vanished. We are humus.

"*Forte! Forte! Fortissimo!*"

"Mother of God, keep us in your care, they're going to kill each other!"

The paving stones were grey, just the same grey as Vladimir Ilyich – he was made by Muscovite sculptor Sergei Merkurov, famous for his stone Lenins the length and breadth of the country. I was doggedly refusing to look at the statue, but even so it was there before my eyes: in his hands he was crumpling his already crumpled cap, and he was stuck on a pedestal that looked like a chimney, gazing down with the expression of a convict. Someone had spilled a bucket of red paint on his plinth: it reminded me of everything I preferred to forget.

"Out! Out! Out!" they weren't quite shouting nor quite sobbing, more and more softly. This was a great day – even Zygmunt Gorgolewski had come to sit on a grey paving stone amid the spectators, with an unlit cigar between his lips.

"All over before it's begun," he repeated mechanically. "Before it's begun. Begun. Gun."

"What do you think about it?" I asked, without opening my mouth. "Are you pleased? Well, of course you are. But you've spent so many years beside each other, you and Lenin. Like under one roof in a communal flat."

"Why are you sitting on the bare ground? Have you gone mad? You'll be sick! You'll die!" shrieked Aba, pulling me by the arm.

"Are you alive?" I said in amazement, like someone with post-traumatic stress disorder, although I didn't know that term yet.

"It's a good thing the child is here. She won't see this on television!" someone said nearby.

I tore my plimsolls free of the ground and took off up a tree. When I was six, Mama made me a medal for climbing trees. A round piece of cardboard, with three black branches on it, and a golden cat in the middle, with every hair in his tail sticking upwards. I still have the medal to this day – it's lying under glass on my desk. You never got one like it, Mr Gorgolewski.

"What are you doing up there? You'll fall and break your neck!"

I looked out for Chornovil, but instead of him a man in a rumpled suit scrambled onto the crane. He read something from a sheet of paper, but the loudspeaker had packed up, and nobody could understand a word of it.

"He's listing the major crimes of communism," said the Intercessor, weeping.

The singing fell silent. And then came the final ascent of the baton. The pick-up. *One-two-three-heaaave!*

In the first second, the leader of the world proletariat hung suspended in the air like a large bell incapable of emitting any sound, and then he fell with a crash into the bed of a lorry painted blue with a large sign saying "People". Everyone clapped: those on the ground and me up in my tree. Justice had been done, now the brave new era would set in. Now we could go home.

Then there was a new clap of thunder, and at once I thought of Gorgolewski – it wasn't the first time he had felt the Opera shake, and now it was crumbling, following in the wake of Lenin, the stone figures were flying head-first from their alcoves – the blindfolded allegory of Tragedy, and corpulent Comedy.

"Let's go home!"

"It's all right, it's just a slab that fell off the plinth, several slabs, I think."

"They're gravestones. Polish and Jewish. Taken from Yanivsky cemetery from the tombs of the Sich Riflemen. How did they get there?"

As the gravestones fell from the plinth, the bones and skulls of citizens of various ethnicities murdered by the regime came tumbling after; they struck the ground and turned back into living young people, who went off to their homes and families, while the idol bowed low, fell down and crumbled to dust. The same thing will happen when they banish the corpse from Red Square – whole villages and towns will come tumbling from under it, masses of people in prison clothing, marked with bullet wounds, will appear in the streets, and then there'll be Judgement Day, and the separation into sheep and goats. A solo voice will ring out: we are humus, but there won't be any need to fertilise the soil.

"Gold! There's gold in there! The communists hid it in the plinth!"

Mrs Intercessor shoved Aba out of the way and dashed off to the front, I helped Aba to stay upright, the boys in uniforms formed a tight chain around the breach left by the leader, and the slabs were loaded onto another lorry, which, just like the first, drove off in an unknown direction. As Aba and I fought our way through to the exit, I held her swollen hand; the puffed-up veins on it were like a map of the Soviet Union with the places marked where they hadn't yet got rid of their statues of Lenin. Around us, bottles of Stolichnaya appeared, people drank straight from them, and passed them from hand to hand. Different groups were singing different folk songs all at once – nobody needed a conductor anymore. We were going in the wrong direction, for the crowd ahead of us was thickening – we were cast out right at the spot where Lenin had been standing minutes earlier. There were no soldiers now; all I could see was a guy with his flies undone, down in the fresh pit, watering it with a copious stream of urine. I caught Aba's accusing gaze on me: I shouldn't have seen that, in an instant I'd change into a pillar of salt. Dearest Aba, I answered her without words, my mind is occupied right now by Zygmunt Gorgolewski, I feel so very sad for him, I really don't know why, but any moment now I'm going to burst out crying. But in fact it was Aba who furtively wiped away tears of emotion, and as we were heading home down Lenin Avenue, she said: "Thou shalt not bow down to idols nor serve them. The word of God has come true, and we are witnesses to that."

I eagerly nodded to confirm this truth, while also feeling the undone safety pin, which had slipped from the collar of my jacket and pierced the fabric of my sweater, and was now digging into my skin somewhere in the region of my ribcage.

The Studio 2

We crossed a few roads and found ourselves on Leo Tolstoy Street, we descended the steps to the basement, then carefully locked the door behind us and lay down on a sofa covered with a dandelion-patterned bedspread, as the gramophone needle penetrated the black lake of the record. Briefly, I regained my voice; several times I said we shouldn't, we needn't, it's wrong, I refuse, I can't, I don't know. I didn't like this sort of prattle, and it wasn't to his taste either – he turned to face the wall, silenced the music with one mighty flick, then got up from the sofa, and began to play the old piano. He was hitting the keys so hard that I was afraid he was going to press them inside it, and then we'd have to call in a professional, I'd have nothing to pay with, I'd go out into the frosty street alone, I'd die in a gateway, because I'd have nothing to go home for either. Mykola went on improvising more and more jazzily, and started murmuring to himself: "*Kul-ba-ba! Kul-ba-ba! Kul-ba-ba!*"

The bedspread was stiff and damp, as I lay on my back, rowing to the beat of his tune, the buoys were ever further away, the lighthouses had vanished over the horizon, the lifeguards had long since gone on leave; with my own hands I pulled off my old woollen sweater, my shapeless grey vest and my faded grey bra, turned onto my stomach, and fantasised that my bare back was growing dandelions, and that's what he was singing about – that's what *kulbaba* means in Ukrainian – a meadow full of dandelions in spring, one flower for every freckle, and every single one of them swaying to the beat along with me. Dandelion – some people call it milk-witch.

"*Kul-ba-ba! Kul-ba-ba! Kul-ba-ba!*"

The tune picked up speed, the dandelions changed into fluffy white clocks, Mykola was blowing off the seeds with his rapid breathing, and my back was transformed into a cemetery, bristling with the hairless heads of dandelion clocks instead of crosses.

"*Kul-ba-ba-ba-ba-ba-ba!*"

That was an unexpected knock at the door, although we hadn't heard any footsteps in advance. He threw a dirty dressing gown over me and gave me a gentle push towards the grand piano – I was to crouch behind it, to hide out of sight. I squeezed in, with my back against the rows of books on the lower shelves of the bookcase; I am a pocket-sized woman, and I can't think which of those words I find more disparaging: "pocket-sized" or "woman". He let his mother in, and her gaze prowled around the walls; she had brought him a hot dinner, he was angry with her, and immediately sent her packing, as though he found the mere presumption that he might feel hunger humiliating, just like the thought that he'd been born from a woman. I sat on the floor with my eyes fixed on the spot where the front of the dressing gown parted ways, gazing at my own nipples. "Milk ducts" – that's what they were called in the medical books. "Milk ducts", from which not a single drop of milk had ever flowed. Milk duct. Milk-witch. *Kulbaba*.

His mother left, locking all the doors behind her, and we lay down together again; Mykola pulled off his trousers, his legs were long and thin, like stilts, depriving him of gravitas, normally this feature was veiled by clothing. I also saw that he was wearing blue cotton long johns – maybe he really had been a child once upon a time. But now those spindly legs of his were the nest for a wild animal – it was rearing up beneath the cover of the long johns, he had to hold it back manually to stop it from lunging forward and tearing me apart.

That is sin, I thought, unable to avert my gaze.

"Would you like me to acquaint you with my intimate parts?" he asked in his usual lecturer's tone.

Hesitantly I nodded, and then he slid a hand into the cave and opened the door from inside; there behind it the beast was lurking, I could see its quivering skin and its disconcerting orifice. Throughout the object lesson, he gently stroked its head.

"This is the scrotum, which holds the testes. Here's the glans, known as the foreskin. You pee through here. And what's happening now is called an erection."

That is sin – the words kept pounding in my head, preventing me from taking in this new information. The spot in between my legs was flooded with heat – I was afraid it showed, I must surely be ringed by a red glow down there, any moment now he'll notice it and declare that I'm a fallen woman.

"Can you possibly be a virgin?"

"I go to the Cathedral, don't I?"

"My generation grew up without God. Nobody talked to us about Him."

"But now you know."

"I was baptised a few years ago."

"You don't behave like the converts – you don't go to church."

"I don't regard the physical expression of love as sinful."

I extracted my face from the folds of the damp bedspread, reached out my hands, and stroked him like a cat, though he smelled like a dog; I wanted him to let me plunge my fingers into his rough fur, close his eyes and sink into a purring state of bliss, I wanted us to stay like that, sharing the delight that the closeness of another body provides, but he had his own plans, he was off in quite another direction, although our interlaced bodies seemed to imply that we were going in the same one. I sank my fingers in him to model him like clay, but they met a mountain sliding onto them, even the mountains obey him, he's as high and mighty as Hoverla, I banged into it painfully, and he got inside me like plaster into a mould, without asking if I wanted to be a statue of myself.

"Take off those earrings," he said. "They're as kitschy as your paintings."

I unhooked the brightly coloured gems that I was very fond of, and tossed them to the floor, while he continued his tour of my body, for which he needed no companion. Why is he so consumed by my body, my pitiful brother ass, that desires nothing but stroking and hugging, I wondered, and suddenly he cried out like a man who has just discovered a long-lost item, he squealed with his eyes shut, pressing my hand to his moist member, as if expecting me to pass a test in the knowledge I had gained about its structure. Moments later he declared in the tone of a lecturer again: "That's what ejaculation is like."

He put on his long johns, got up, went into the kitchenette, and tipped three heaped teaspoonfuls of Fort coffee into an Italian espresso machine, standing with his back to me until the hot drink began to hiss its way through into the upper chamber. He poured it into two china cups with thick sides, and silently handed me one.

It was dark and frosty when we went outside, and we slipped on lumps of dirty ice, my hand in his pocket, his hand in his pocket. I did everything I could to sneak stealthily down the streets, which were full of his students and friends – the times were over when I'd plodded along with my eyes fixed on the mouldering heads of Polish poets set into alcoves on the upper storeys of buildings – now the streets had become an obstacle course, and my suspicious gaze was a scout, whom now and then I sent out far ahead of me. Mykola, as ever, strode along without haste.

We stopped at a house in the area near the Polytechnic – eclecticism, note the round turrets right at the top – entered a gateway covered in white stucco – diligent execution, zero artistic value – and crossed a courtyard packed with little Zaporozhets cars that had taken root; they were protected by tarpaulin covers, and I could have done with one too, because the sky had started to spit out sheets of wet snow – my hands were on my head, his hands were on my head – the courtyard took us to another gateway – look at the wrought-iron letterbox, some cretin has coated it in brown oil paint – and from there we entered another courtyard, where I saw an outhouse roofed in tin, the hail was drumming on its roof, making holes right through it, and making holes in our hatless heads too. We knocked at a door, which was opened by a middle-aged man with wisps of black hair on either side of his bald skull; with a keen glance he instantly registered our interwoven hands. We entered a room so densely packed with heads that there was nowhere to put one's own; standing together on a long table, with necks and without, shiny and matt, of stone and of wood, all of them instantly turned towards me and set about inspecting me – their eye sockets showed no mercy for my sin. Amid these dead heads, our host's bald one trembled as he fixed a drink to welcome us. He set a small ladder against a wall unit and climbed up to the ceiling to fetch some carboys down from a shelf; in the process his head jostled a whole forest of legs that was growing there: straight and crossed, of stone and of metal, all of them bare. The wardrobe next to them was decorated with paper Virgin Marys in golden crowns, and a likeness of the Ukrainian future prime minister Viktor Yushchenko. Mykola and our host sat down facing it and poured cloudy wine into glasses from a carboy covered with basketwork. I drank too, and after the very first sips the heads began to overlap: the host was superimposed on the Virgin Mary of Yazlovets, Mykola's hair on the host's hair, Mykola's hair on the host's bald pate, Mykola's hair on the bald pates of the lifeless heads, every last one of which looked like Taras Shevchenko, the national bard, with heavy brows drooping over bulging eyes, long moustaches drooping too, and ribbons hanging from their cross-stitched shirts. Mykola and our host were discussing a tricky issue to do with the approaching faculty conference, grumbling about the dean and making notes on the backs of pages full of writing, while I sipped the opaque liquid, wine from Serednie in sunny Transcarpathia, which matures in splendid cellars built by the Turks four hundred years ago. All the heads were just the same, though not entirely –

I noticed one with a bald top and a drooping brow, but with no moustache, look out, an interloper! I wonder how he barged his way in here? I stared at him more intently – we'd met somewhere before, and it hadn't been a pleasant experience; I kept lapping up the wine like water as I tried to remember the exact quote from *Ruslan and Lyudmila* when the unhappy knight is searching for his sweetheart in the open fields, but instead of her he encounters a giant head:

> . . . *our valiant prince*
> *stared – at a sight beyond belief!*
> *How to describe by word or palette?*
> *Before him was a living Head,*
> *the enormous eyes shut tight in sleep.*[1]

Ruslan coped with it, I thought, for when the head began to blow on him and threw him off his horse, when it started shouting and taunting him with its awful tongue, by way of self-defence he quickly and nimbly stabbed it with his lance, whereas I was defenceless, and hungry too; my eyes sought something to eat, but the only thing on the table was red viburnum berry preserve, sour and bitter – Aba always gave me a teaspoonful of it to relieve a sore throat. Mykola and our host were debating problems with the dean, loudly tut-tutting about his senile dementia, or maybe it was the viburnum – the hard skins stuck to my teeth and tongue, it was difficult to unstick and then chew them. The intruder-head had camouflaged itself very well amid the busts of Shevchenko – he had pushed his way in

1 Alexander Pushkin, *Ruslan and Lyudmila*, third canto, ll. 234–8, trans. Roger Clarke.

between the bard's cherry orchards, exploited the peasant women and Cossack rebels sharpening their scythes, but that was nothing compared with the dozen Christs crucified without crosses, up against the ceiling, I wonder if he ever glances in their direction, or casts his soundless atheistic anathemas at them?

"Where did that head come from?" I asked softly.

Our host winked at me, topped up the wine and blithely switched to the new topic. He spoke about the summer of 1990 and the officer's wives protesting outside the Opera against the removal of the statue, about the Jewish gravestones found inside the plinth and the sculptor Merkurov – it seems he was the only member of the Moscow freemason's lodge to be lucky enough to die a natural death. He tacked on the legend about the apparent suicide of Gorgolewski, the architect, because the theatre had subsided – neither I, nor Mykola corrected him, but fleetingly we exchanged meaningful glances – finally he came to the moment when the blue lorry carrying the deposed statue of Lenin was steered into the backyard of one of the local factories, and in the presence of very few witnesses was placed face to the ground. Despite this, news of the overthrown leader of the world proletariat quickly ran around the city, and delegations of curious onlookers began to visit the factory. Finally, a special commission was sent from Kiev, who pronounced that the "conditions for storing Ilyich were far from satisfactory". That was exactly how they put it – for those were times when although you could dismantle Lenin, you could not yet cover him in mud. So he had to be got rid of in a civilised, inexpensive way, and shortly after, a second execution was held in a quiet corner, not as pompous as the previous one. Lenin's head was knocked off, the torso was set aside for a monument to the victims of communist repression and, for the time being, he was put away in a warehouse.

"How did the head end up in your possession?" I asked, but our host just laughed and poured me more wine, though I hadn't yet managed to finish the round before, so my glass began to overflow, which he found even funnier; he made a dreadful face, clapping himself on his football-sized knees. I didn't know how to make him start to sing, and so I asked him: "How do you feel as you wipe the dust off it?"

"I don't wipe the dust off it. I wipe my feet on it," he replied, sniggering.

Mykola's face twitched with distaste, Yushchenko came down from the wall and superimposed himself on it, and Lenin's squinting eyes replaced those of our host, who turned them on me and rasped: "I know who you are – you're Marianna's daughter."

The glass overturned, the undrunk Transcarpathian wine spilled down my jeans, my interlocutor leaped up and tried to wipe me with a red cloth, peering caringly into my eyes. He'd been at the heart of events that day, he confessed, he'd sung "The Red Viburnum" loud enough to make his throat sore, he had a cousin who'd heard the shots himself, two or three of them, when exactly was it – in July or August? I switched off and got stuck in the tedious mire seeping from the cloud of my mother's laudable martyrdom and of dense smoke from the cigarettes that both men were smoking; I had nothing to say about that story, they knew it all better than I did, as our host became more and more moved by his own reminiscences: Marianna was truly the reincarnation of Solomiya Krushelnytska, the same sonorous mezzo-soprano, Ukrainian in every fibre of her being. Incidentally, he himself had for some time been planning to publish a genuinely patriotic cultural magazine, but didn't know how to find a sponsor, and was in two minds about the title. Would "Independence" be better, or "The Red Viburnum" – what did we think?

"We've known each other for years," said Mykola, once we were back in the courtyard. "I owe him a lot: he got me into the college, he urged me to do my doctorate. But it's also a fact that he used to specialise in busts of Lenin."

Up to our knees in fresh snow, we waded across the connecting courtyards, my head on his shoulder, his head on my head, both trying and failing to chew the bitter berries we'd been served.

"All the best to you and your student," said our host to Mykola in parting, and now I couldn't shake off the impression that after these words his gaze, which skittered in my direction, had burned a mark on my face.

The Casket

The snow was almost gone by now; in odd places our feet still slipped on dirty lumps of it, mine in little pink knee boots, Aba's in black lace-ups with solid heels, and Mama's in white felt winter boots, the colour of the snowdrops now being sold on every corner of our street. Those simple flowers weren't right for today's festivity, so we went to Halytska Square.

"It's not spring yet, the weather's still very changeable," Aba said crabbily. "You must put on a hat. And warm winter footwear. You must take care of yourself."

"What if I can't stand this self of mine?" asked Mama, whether joking or being serious I don't know. "What if I want to finish the bitch off?"

As I'd known for ages, there were two women living inside Mama, one of whom hated the other.

The flower ladies were standing right by the entrance to the square – first came hyacinths and daffodils, then beyond them, under a roof, carnations and roses. We went further in for a large bouquet of carnations in stiff plastic wrapping that looked like glass.

"I can't bear these petty bourgeois get-togethers!" Mama said.

"Aren't you ashamed, Marianna?" said Aba, bristling. "Have some respect! And gratitude!"

The cars speeding through the puddles on Ivan Franko Street whipped up silver tsunamis in a golden frame of spring sunlight. As we waited at the stop for a number two tram, I gazed up the slope of Lenin Street, imagining that it led to the sea, or some other wonderful place where I had never been. In fact, our tram went past the grey Saint Anthony's Catholic church, then the white Orthodox Saints Peter and Paul; soon after we got off at a spot where, outside the square block of an unfamiliar place of worship, stood a green tank with its barrel pointing towards us. We sought out the apartment building named "Our Standard"; the one next to it, named "Leninism", was no longer ours. Three steps led up to the entrance, two low and one high. Aba's legs had no trouble clearing the low ones, but they stopped at the high one. Turning to place one foot sideways on, she feebly tried raising it to the necessary height. Leaning on our arms, she closed her eyes and wobbled, until finally she managed to propel her small body upwards; a layer of moisture appeared on her smooth, barely wrinkled brow.

Unlike anywhere else, the stairwell in this block was bright and clean, with cactuses in pots on each floor and even a sort of carpeting on the stairs. A modern lift roared away like the factories on shift-work throughout our boundless socialist motherland.

Uncle Alexei, brother of my long deceased grandfather, and his wife, Auntie Maria, were waiting for us in the doorway. They were wearing festive faces, which, just like their Sunday best, they had put on specially for today's party – I had seen the other kind they wore on the one occasion when we had happened to bump into them in town. Once we had exchanged greetings, presented the flowers and a gift – a heavy ceramic vase wrapped in newspaper – Uncle Alexei removed each of our coats with the gesture of a connoisseur of the fairer sex. He had long, sparse hair carefully combed back and a large, oval paunch that he carried solemnly before him, as if its contents were priceless. He was in a light, starched shirt and a pair of suit trousers. His welcoming kiss filled me with disgust: his wet lips sucked in a bit of my cheek, and for a brief moment gently chewed on it; afterwards it was impolite to wipe myself clean. Auntie Maria had an ample belly too, swathed in a grey, belted woollen dress, and seemed entirely made of dry paper – she kissed the air instead of me. Uncle Alexei and Auntie Maria had no children of their own, and Mama was Uncle Alexei's only niece; for as long as I could remember, we went to his birthday party every year.

In the willow-green light of the hall, Auntie Maria fetched out some slippers from the closet – all in good condition, all from abroad. Also new were the books in the glass-fronted cases lining the walls, arranged by the colour of their spines, with the works of Lenin in dark blue covers standing at the top.

"Dear friends, please come inside!"

We stepped hesitantly along the flooring, which was like the well-baked crust of a sponge cake scented with lemon and vanilla, then entered the sitting room, where we were flooded with brilliance and heat. Mirrors and chandeliers, candles and silverware, a full table in the middle, and around it the guests – older and younger gentlemen in suits, and ladies of various ages, going bald and with permanent waves. The older generation included Uncle Alexei's wartime comrades, with whom he had fought at Stalingrad and Kursk, Kraków and Berlin. When I was younger, I had refused to believe that my fat uncle had ever been a soldier, so at one of the previous parties, to his guests' amusement, he had taken off his trousers to show me the uneven dents in his leg where the bullets had penetrated; I, like doubting Thomas, had put a finger in each of them in turn.

On the table the appetisers were waiting: eggs stuffed with mushrooms and mayonnaise, red and black caviar canapés, beetroot and prune salad, the Olivier salad mandatory at every Soviet feast, home-made marinated roast peppers, tomatoes and cucumbers, herrings and dill pickle, thinly sliced yellow cheese and various kinds of sausage, with large and small lumps of fat. On the windowsill stood bottles of wine and champagne, vodka and brandy, Borzhomi mineral water and orangeade.

The guests were sitting in light, modern chairs and armchairs below a shining display cabinet, and also on a springy sofa with a thin kilim draped over it. Among them was Violette – I had already heard her voice from the corridor. She was Uncle Alexei's "favourite goddaughter", which didn't refer to a church sacrament, but to the close ties for which Soviet people sometimes borrowed religious terminology. Curiously, she and Mama were born on the same day in the same year, and each one played a special role in Uncle Alexei's life: Mama was his only niece, and Violette was the daughter of his closest friend and comrade-in-arms who, like my grandfather, was no longer alive.

"Dearest Uncle, do sit down!" Violette hooted in her deep voice. "Let's raise a toast to congratulate the birthday boy!"

Although these were appropriate, neutral words, I couldn't shake off the impression that Violette was faking.

"Ah, who's this? Our *artistochka!*" she disdainfully remarked as soon as Mama appeared.

For as long as I had known her, "Violette", as I called her, had coloured her hair, lips and fingernails purple, which was why I had thought up this nickname; at this particular party she was even wearing an open mohair cardigan of the same hue. Mama sat facing her across the table, Aba joined the other old folks at its head, and I took advantage of the commotion to go into the bedroom.

There in the middle stood a mighty double bed, covered with a sort of frilly drape – an icebreaker in lace – and of such a height that you needed special steps to scramble onto it. I crumpled the pillows, but I hadn't the courage to get on top. Over the bed hung a black-and-white photograph, a portrait of a young couple with glittering eyes and white-toothed smiles – I didn't know who they were. There weren't many things surrounding it: a bedside table with a handful of pills in a cut-glass bowl, a heavy wardrobe, an elegant suit rack and a dressing table. There were some ornamental porcelain figurines on the windowsill, including a dog with the rag of a shot-down duck in its mouth, dancing ballerinas and a doll's house – I rearranged them all my own way. I opened the dressing-table drawers, took out weighty strings of pearls, solid gold earrings and shiny cufflinks, and tried each of them on in turn before the mirror, though none of them was to my liking. Then I reached for the perfumes in large and small flasks, and sniffed at them with repulsion – they made me think of the words "cognac" and "restaurant". From the bedroom window, I could see a long flight of steps leading somewhere towards the Kaiserwald woods – we had never been down them, because of Aba's bad legs.

"To your very good health, dear Uncle Alexei!"

"Your very good health!"

"Quite so, good health is what matters most!"

From one of the dressing-table drawers, I took out a small black casket. It was exactly the same as the one Aba had, with the profile of a man with a prominent nose engraved on the lid. Auntie Maria's casket was locked and I couldn't see the key anywhere.

"Chopin!" Aba would often sigh, and from the tone of her voice I knew it was a matter of the greatest gravity.

I went back into the sitting room and spooned some marinated peppers onto my plate. I fancied a drop of the champagne that the adults were drinking, and asked Mama to let me try some.

"Make a wish. You should always make a wish when you try something for the very first time," she whispered as she handed me her glass.

Just one wish – it would have to be something big. For Aba to be well again? To be lucky in love? For the fall of the Soviet Union?

At the table the news was being reported: from the factory where Uncle Alexei was deputy director, and from the hospital, where Auntie Maria worked as a nurse.

The topic of the two landscapes painted in oils that had recently been hung on the sitting-room wall made a brief appearance too – everyone praised them.

"I think they're too gloomy, they lack lightness and air," said Aba.

After this remark a heavy silence fell, and I was filled with shame, possibly because Aba had spoken with her mouth full, or maybe because nobody here regarded her as an expert.

"But then I could be wrong . . . They really are nice pictures!"

Now I felt ashamed of her for backtracking so easily. In this house she was often timid and submissive. I looked at her closely – she didn't fit in with the crystal glasses, the furniture and the ladies here, although these ladies showed greater signs of wear and tear; they had deeper wrinkles and thinner hair, yet Aba lacked the artificial sheen that they had assumed for the festive occasion, to be hung up in the wardrobe again with their clothing once it was over. She was the same as ever, in her shabby halo and her badly ironed dress.

"I'd like to propose a toast to your dear wife!" someone exclaimed. "To your loyal comrade-in-arms and in long years of peace. Your health, Maria!"

Unnoticed, I slipped back into the bedroom.

In her casket Aba kept papers, drawings and letters which she sometimes showed me, but she took great care to lock it afterwards. What Auntie Maria kept in hers, I had no idea. Both little boxes dated back to very remote times, when Uncle Alexei the soldier and Auntie Maria the army nurse fought against the fascists, to liberate first the cities of Russia, then of Ukraine, followed by the Polish ones, Lwów and Kraków. Along the way Lwów – soon to be Soviet Lvov – had been so much to their liking that they'd decided to settle here for life, and Uncle Alexei had invited his younger brother, my future grandfather, to join him. Except that before she met Grandpa, Aba had had Chopin. He was part of Poland, the one that existed fully and really in Lwów before the war – for at the time who could have believed the border shifts would be permanent? The gentlemen still wore hats and kissed the ladies on the hand, the priests celebrated the Catholic Mass, and instead of Lenin the central promenade was graced by a bronze statue of King Jan Sobieski, whom the strangers from the East had mistaken for Bogdan Khmelnitsky. In those post-war years, Aba had found a distant relative, a distinguished professor of medicine who lived in a beautiful villa on Kastelówka Street. Their common surname was unusual, the girl was charming and totally committed to returning to her roots, so the professor started inviting her to his home, to gatherings of people involved in art and culture. At one of them she met Chopin – I don't know what he was really called; from half statements and allusions all I knew was that he was a pianist and had a prominent nose. Later on he had withdrawn to the West, just like his movable homeland. They hadn't taken Aba with them.

"Cheers! Your very good health," cried the guests, raising their glasses, while Auntie Maria bashfully dropped her gaze and filled their plates. I stood a while in the sitting-room doorway, then crossed into the kitchen. Here some large bowls lay in waiting, full of other goodies, including home-made pelmenis, slices of roast meat, mashed potato, schnitzels, and also a pot of borscht. On top of the kitchen cabinets, too high for me to reach, sat the items demanding the longest wait: a Pischinger torte, crescent-shaped pastries filled with rose-petal jam, tubes filled with caramel cream, short-pastry tarts and a large, walnut layer cake covered with a protective sheet of silver foil. From the kitchen window I could see the trams speeding down Lenin Street, and in their wake some tanks flashed by, first the one Uncle Alexei had driven in his youth, then the one that stood on a plinth outside the block. I opened the doors of a small white cupboard; on the top shelf stood a row of little alabaster elephants, smooth and enticing. They were arranged in line from largest to smallest, but I soon disturbed their order. Noticing an electric samovar next to the cupboard, I lifted its lid – it was full of water with whitish streaks in it.

I went into the corridor. One of the glazed bookcase doors was open, and there stood Mama, reading. I sat down next to her, picked up a magazine called "The Woman Worker", and for a while we both read in silence. From the sitting room we could hear Violette's voice like the trumpets of Jericho – she was talking about the school where she worked; I bet she whacks the children on the hands with a ruler, I thought. Her husband, a fragile-looking man with dark hair, rarely raised his head from his plate and only spoke up if it was unavoidable. I knew from Mama that he was a high-ranking K.G.B. officer.

"Come and have the second course!"

We returned to the sitting room. It was stuffy and noisy in there, the guests' faces had gone red, and by now someone had managed to spill wine on the tablecloth and sprinkle salt on the stain. Uncle Alexei was going around the table, filling the glasses with the gesture of a seasoned toastmaster; wet patches were spreading under the arms of his shirt.

"To peaceful skies overhead!"

Clink-clink went the crystal glasses tapping together. Peace is the main thing – the guests at these gatherings often repeated that phrase, especially the ones who had lived through the war.

"To the hell of war never happening again!"

Peace by all means, but not at the cost of freedom – that was what Aba had heard from Chopin, whose older brother had liberated the city he called Lwów shoulder to shoulder with Uncle Alexei, though they never had the chance to meet. Uncle Alexei had arrived too late to see the red-and-white Polish flag flying over the Town Hall,

161

because it was only there for a very short time. And Chopin's brother, along with all the other Polish Home Army men, was cheated by Uncle Alexei's commanders, disarmed and thrown into an N.K.V.D. dungeon. Chopin was left with a portrait of him on his desk.

The hot dishes were served on beautiful china plates with a subtle rose pattern. I defended myself like a partisan against the onslaught of food, but nobody would listen to me; Auntie Maria shoved under my nose a ruddy chicken leg wrapped in sticky, pimply skin. I cast a meaningful glance at Aba – would she be able to take over my plate without being noticed?

"Bandera's men have begun to raise their voices," Violette said suddenly, disdainfully branding the Ukrainian independence campaigners with the wartime nationalist leader's name. "Have they really forgotten what a rough ride our boys gave them after the war?"

"Who? Who's that?" asked Aba, who hadn't heard her properly.

"The locals," said Violette. "The fascist stooges."

The locals. So she used that word too, and just like Great-Granma she uttered it in a special tone of voice – containing fear, but also scorn. Without having to look up, I knew what was bound to happen. Mama was like an Amazonian in a flowing cloak, her sword was quick to slash and merciless – nothing could have stopped it.

"The locals?" she asked. "They're at home. But nobody invited you here. You're the invaders."

In the silence that fell after this remark, we could hear her footsteps and the crash of the front door as it opened and then closed.

"Dearest Uncle, I ask you!" Violette whined plaintively, and then instantly screamed: "You lying bitch!"

"I do beg your pardon!" said Aba ardently, and slowly left the room.

I sat with my head hung low, studying the weave of the kilim covering the sofa.

"Are all your glasses full?" asked Uncle Alexei. "I'd like to propose a toast to our dear guests. May harmony ever prevail in this house, and may we keep meeting here like this for many years to come!"

Clink-clink, and with a sense of relief, the guests went back to their interrupted conversations, Uncle Alexei sat down in his place of honour, threw a glass of brandy down his throat, and chased it with a meat cutlet.

He and Auntie Maria had been tolerably satisfied with his brother's choice: an unassuming girl with a medical diploma. Cautious and circumspect, they had only attended the civil wedding, pretending to be unaware of the church ceremony, which took place one afternoon at Mary Magdalene's, one of the last to be performed there before it was converted into a polytechnic students' club. Later on, each year they met up on their birthdays, at our home or at theirs. While Uncle Alexei held ever more senior posts at hospitals and factories, Grandpa climbed higher and higher up the rungs of the military, and ran the garrison orchestra. The less hair the brothers had on their heads, the more ample their paunches and their festive tables became. Even when Grandpa fell sick with depression and began to spend all day in a darkened room, the birthdays remained the one and only occasion for which he put on an ironed shirt and a celebratory face. Whereas, after her marriage, Aba was no longer invited to parties at the professor of medicine's villa – the reason was given in the form of a discreet allusion: the point was that she had married a Russian. But good God, why had Chopin left for Poland without her?

When Auntie Maria began to clear the dirty plates and glasses, the women leaped from their seats to help her, and the men stood up too; the flurry of activity brought everyone relief, and I went into the kitchen as well, to join in with drying the dishes. By the window stood a large, shapeless old crone – Violette's mother, and I heard her saying to another lady: "I remember when she wanted to go to Chile to support the communists fighting against Pinochet. And now she's in with Bandera's lot!" And the old crone tapped her forehead non-stop until she noticed that I was looking at her.

Once darkness had fallen outside, dessert was served in the sitting room, where Uncle Alexei lit the fancy chandeliers, poured coffee into some little gilded cups, and offered liqueurs to go with it. The television was switched on – there was coverage of the hockey championships.

"Somebody sent Alexei these cassettes from Poland. Frankly, they're nothing special! The girls dance nicely, they've got long legs, but when they take off their bras they've nothing to show. Just bee stings! Nature has endowed our Russian girls more generously."

Well, well, I was surprised to discover that Auntie Maria was so very laid-back; Aba would never have watched a tape of that kind. I cast a glance in her direction: she had come back into the sitting room, and was heartily tucking into a piece of cake, while also saying something to the woman next to her, crumbs flying from her mouth.

I had long since noticed that merely alluding to sexual matters prompted anger or embarrassment in Aba. Nor was I capable of imagining her in the role of a young woman in love, even less as the sort of girl who tries to determine her own fate. It must have gone something like this:

"Mama, he has asked for my hand and I want to marry him."

"That two-bit musician? Out of the question."

"But Mama, why?"

"You think you can go abroad? Abandon your mother for ever? Is that how you're going to repay me for everything I've done for you?"

The young Aba, with lovely bright eyes and fit, strong legs sank to the floor as if lifeless. We have a single heart, Great-Grandma often used to tell her, which meant that Aba had no right to a heart of her own. To thank her mother for letting her have her wartime bread, Aba had to sacrifice her own life in return. She broke up with Chopin, remained in the city that now became Lvov, and grew heavy and clumsy, the opposite of what happens in "The Nutcracker".

Not in the least put out, Violette was loudly expatiating on the new reform which meant that the standard course at primary schools would continue for a year longer. After smoking a fag on the stairs, Mama had come back in, and was now sitting in the hall with a volume of Chekhov on her knees.

I ate my dessert and went to join her. She continued reading, while I opened the door of the closet and examined Uncle Alexei's jacket, which was hanging up inside. It was dark, almost black, worn shiny on the elbows, and fitted to the size of his paunch. I gave it a quick sniff – it smelled of sweat and metal – and then I tested how very heavy it was. There wasn't a patch of bare fabric on its front; it was entirely covered in military honours, decorations and medals. On the right side, there were some red-and-gold stars with inscriptions such as "For the defence of Kursk", and on the left some lighter little gold discs hanging on striped ribbons. Also on the right, in the spot where children usually draw the heart, there was a row of longer and shorter ribbon bars – testimony to wounds sustained at the front. I know that each year, on May 9, Uncle Alexei donned this jacket, Auntie Maria put on a navy-blue dress that was also decorated with medals, and together they went to the nearby Hill of Glory, the Soviet soldiers' burial ground. There they paid a visit to Violette's father and other comrades lying at rest, bringing them armfuls of red tulips wrapped in stiff paper; at some of the gravesides their cheeks became moist. I also know that afterwards a party similar to today's was held at Uncle Alexei and Auntie Maria's flat, to which we were not invited.

After coffee it was time to say goodbye. Our hosts escorted us to the door, politely waiting for us to find our boots, and then Uncle Alexei unhurriedly helped each of us into our coats. Nothing on his or Auntie Maria's face implied that they were upset with Mama for today's incident.

"Thank you for coming!" they repeated with no disappointment. "Please come again!"

After the farewell kisses we ended up in the stairwell. I remembered that on the way in it had been flooded with sunlight, but now total darkness reigned. This contrast, and also a bloated feeling from overeating made me regret the irretrievably wasted day.

"Help me!" said Aba to Mama. Going downstairs was even harder for her than going up.

We passed the tank, barely visible now, and reached Lenin Street. Mama raised her right hand, and soon after a battered black Volga pulled up beside us; its smooth seats smelled of tobacco. Aba sat in front beside the whiskered driver, with Mama and me in the back. The car raced down the hill, braking only once at the traffic lights on Lenin Square.

When I went back there later on, I stopped at the very same lights, but now the square was called Vynnykivsky, the street name had been changed back to Lychakivska, and the battered black car was a Chevrolet.

I didn't know the woman who answered the door of Uncle Alexei and Auntie Maria's flat; she let me inside and instantly disappeared – I heard her talking on a mobile in another room. I lit the flickering willow-green lamp in the hall, put on the same slippers as ever, cast an eye at the unaltered arrangement of books on the shelves and went into the bedroom. Here too, everything was in its place, except that the lacy bedspread had greyed, and there was an open packet of nappies for adults and a small icon in a golden frame on the dressing table. Automatically, I reached for the pillows, and picked one up – it fell apart in my hands, ejecting mouldering feathers through holes in the pillowcase. I put it down and went into the kitchen, opened the cupboard, and swiftly swept the small cluster of elephants into my handbag; just then Violette came in. I hadn't immediately recognised her because she looked as if her former body had been swallowed by an old hag the size of a whale, and now from deep inside it she broadcast in her usual, pedagogical tone: "Thank you for coming. There are things we need to talk about. But first let's have a drink to our reunion!"

In the dust-coated sitting room, the kilim that had once covered the sofa was now lying on it, packed into a plastic bag. Violette opened the drinks cabinet.

"Champagne, wine or brandy?" she asked, and immediately added: "Why am I asking? The brandy's the only one that isn't past its use-by date."

Clink-clink, said the familiar glasses, and it occurred to me that my old champagne wish had come true. Violette had blonde hair now, pearly nail polish and a dark blue ladies' suit with a golden trident, the Ukrainian national emblem, in her lapel.

"I've been teaching the history of Ukraine for ten years," she explained, noticing my gaze. "Still at the same school. I could have retired by now, but I love my job."

She emptied her glass, then took a folder from her handbag.

"Let's get down to brass tacks. I've an offer to put to you. We've inherited this flat jointly, but I don't want to sell it. I've got an idea for it. Look, here's a sort of business plan."

I picked up the folder, which bore the title "Red Homestay Lviv" and read the text, written out in neat calligraphy:

"This flat was the home of a very special couple – a former Red Army soldier and a nurse – where they lived for forty years. A short family history is to be found on the website, and on a notice by the entrance, together with a description of the flat (what is kept where, what you may and may not do). On the shelves you'll find Soviet diplomas (you can pick them up and inspect them), books about Lenin and the Communist Party (you can look at these and read them), a jacket hanging in the cupboard that's covered in medals (you can try it on and take pictures), and there are also some old electric shavers (every Soviet man shaved with one of these), pictures and photos on the walls that create a home-like atmosphere. Additional attractions: a panoramic view of Lviv from the balcony, and excellent transport connections to the city centre.

"Overnight accommodation for three or four (one sofa bed plus one double bed), extra camp beds can also be provided. Price per person per night: 15 Euros.

"Available on request: a festive supper in the style of the Brezhnev era (crystal glasses and bowls, flowers). Dishes: Olivier salad, home-made pelmenis, 'Red Carnation' cake. Price: 15 Euros per person. Alcohol priced separately.

"Appliances: C.D./D.V.D. player with Soviet songs, T-shirts printed with the flat's logo and website address, souvenirs – plastic tanks."

Under this description there was a note: "Target group: young Poles aged 20–35 seeking unconventional leisure activities."

"When it comes to Polish tourists in Lviv, the market is very good right now," said Violette, "and according to the forecasts, it'll keep improving."

In the margin in small letters was added: "Lay ceramic floor tiles – they throw up!" At this point she gave me a knowing wink.

"I'm studying abroad, I'm rarely in Lviv," I stuttered.

"I know, but it doesn't matter, I'll take care of everything. After subtracting expenses and paying off the start-up investments you'll get thirty-five percent a month. I think that's an honest deal."

Clink-clink, said the glasses, more confidently than before.

"I need some time to think about it," I said, my voice shaking. "I'll give you my answer tomorrow."

"No problem," said Violette, and after a pause she asked: "Have you been to the cemetery already?"

"Yes."

"You're lucky to have all of them in Lychakiv," she sighed. "That's the smart place to be. They're going to have golf carts there soon. The one in Holosko's awful. I'll tell you about it – but first we could do with a snack."

She produced two packets of Svitoch crackers and two pots of Jantar processed cheese from her handbag; we carried them and the brandy into the sitting room, put them down on the polished table top, and as we gradually emptied the bottle labelled "Ararat", I listened to Violette's account of what had happened to her last year. She had decided to order a granite memorial for Uncle Alexei's grave, so first she'd had a long journey to the cemetery on several minibuses, then she'd lost her way in the labyrinth of tombstones with life-sized portraits etched on them featuring gypsies in fur hats, then she had sought plot number 40 in vain, because the signs with the numbers had all gone, and so had the pine tree split in two by lightning that was meant to act as a landmark for the spot she was looking for. Finally, she had found the pine tree and also the plot, but there were five times as many graves now, and the entire slope – plot 40 at Holosko lay on an extremely steep incline – was overgrown with giant weeds taller than Violette.

"What did Uncle Alexei die of?" I asked. "I know Auntie Maria had Alzheimer's in her final years . . ."

"Her illness finished them both off. All his life, Uncle Alexei had been waited on by Auntie Maria, but now he had to look after her – and he was neither willing nor able to do that."

Clink-clink, this time more of a humming sound, because Violette had begun to sob; the tears rose to her eyes like the rain in the dark clouds gathering above plot number 40 at Holosko cemetery.

"It was awful: thick scrub full of thorns. I had no shears and no gloves with me. There was a veritable jungle in the spot where Uncle Alexei should have lain. I tore it all out with my bare hands, treading on the other graves. There wasn't a living soul in sight. I was covered in scratches and thorn pricks, I'd come in a blouse with short sleeves and bare feet in sandals. Eventually I realised a storm was closing in."

Was she lamenting the bitter fate of Uncle Alexei and Auntie Maria, I wondered, as I watched the tears streaming erratically down her face, or was she feeling self-pity? But it occurred to me at once that it didn't really matter. I was highly surprised by this thought – it took me aback, and it bid me ignore my embarrassment and stroke Violette's hands, then to refill our glasses and ask after her husband.

"We're not officially divorced, but . . ." she sobbed, "for a good few years now he's been living in Kiev. He's got a high-up post in the security service. He never invites me to visit, I'm on my own."

After a pause she carried on with her story.

"At the cemetery I got a splinter that I didn't notice. My foot began to fester, in this spot right here, just above the ankle. I had to have an urgent procedure, under anaesthetic. The doctor said I could have lost my life."

Once the crackers had been consumed and the bottle emptied, and darkness had fallen outside, we went into the bedroom. Violette spread out Auntie Maria's valuables on the bed. And so, on the deck

171

of the old icebreaker, gold rings with gemstones in various colours appeared, the familiar strings of pearls and the cufflinks, and two massive platinum watches as well.

What an orgy of chutzpah, I thought, gazing at it all.

"Have you seen a small black box with Chopin's profile on it?" I asked.

Instead of answering, with a theatrical gesture Violette pulled out all the dressing-table drawers.

"These fingers have never stolen a thing," she laughed, holding out her hands to me.

Together, we ascended the steps onto the old bed, and slowly drank up the out-of-date champagne, while playing bridge and chatting about this and that, among other things about the poor solution to the question of lighting in Uncle Alexei and Auntie Maria's bedroom: a solitary bulb hanging from the ceiling shone too weakly to disperse the gloom in this large space, and it was impossible to read a single line by the weak glow of the wall lamps fixed on either side of the bed. Nor was it easy to look at the albums full of photos, in which the white-toothed couple was depicted, smiling radiantly in front of various historical monuments in the happiest land on earth, and other socialist countries too, such as Poland, Bulgaria and Mongolia.

"Uncle Alexei was a terrible old lecher," admitted Violette. "He screwed anything that moved. Auntie Maria knew about it, but she turned a blind eye. They had an understanding."

In answer I merely sighed. We went on playing cards.

When I woke up next morning, neither Violette, nor the empty bottles were beside me, but there was a note and some keys on the dressing table. With my fingers, I combed the feathers from my hair and went outside. The sun was shining, the melting snow crunched, I could hear the crack of falling icicles, and trams singing in the distance. I didn't turn towards Lychakivska Street, but went down the steps that led towards Kaiserwald, and on the way I counted them. I thought of a new wish, telling myself it would come true if the total were more than a hundred.

The Underground River

"I'm coming with you!" I told her, as I was in the habit of doing, but this time she agreed without opposition. She had just taken a bath, and was now finishing her make-up in front of the bathroom mirror: holding a little box marked "Leningradski", she spat on a rectangular block of mascara, mixed it with a little brush, and then painted it onto her long lashes – no-one had lashes like Mama's, except Snow White perhaps, but hers were false. The foaming water was forming a whirlpool in the bath, and I felt as if the stream that carried her scent were trying to tell me something, but it was stammering, because the strong current was pushing it under the earth, into the Poltva river, which famously merged with two other underground streams right below our building. We were living on a watershed, despite which the water in the taps was limited – it appeared between six and nine in the morning, and late-risers had to be satisfied with what they could find in buckets and saucepans. The programme for June was lying on the broken washing machine: today, the fourth, they were performing "Carmen", with Marianna Astafieva in the title role.

I heard Aba switching on the television, so I went into the main room.

"Tragedy in Bashkiria . . . " said the newsreader. "Gas leak . . . coaches derailed . . . hundreds of victims . . . serious burns . . . "

"What's happened?" I asked.

"Two trains blew up – there was a gas leak in a pipeline running parallel to the tracks, and as they were passing it exploded. Hundreds of people have been killed."

"Where?"

"Near the city of Ufa."

Standing in the doorway, I saw a picture of coaches thrown off the embankment, ripped-off doors, shattered glass and heaps of twisted metal; suddenly the screen was filled with interference, out of which loomed the face of the popular presenter Vlad Listyev.

"Yesterday, the Moscow Olympic Stadium was bursting at the seams for a concert by the legendary rock group Pink Floyd, making their first ever visit to the Soviet Union . . . " he said.

Coloured stripes swallowed the moustachioed Listyev, and the pictures from Bashkiria returned.

"First Chernobyl and now this explosion," sighed Aba. "What else are we in for?"

I tiptoed into Mama's bedroom, opened her wardrobe, and took out a red miniskirt and black tights. Mama didn't comment on my sartorial innovations, she was busy talking to someone on the telephone, and frowning – even though Aba was always telling her that if she didn't take better care of her facial expressions she'd soon look like an old woman. Once we'd left the flat, she hurried me down the stairs, but on our floor, I froze beside the stained-glass oak tree – the lead frames surrounding it were railway tracks, with two long passenger trains running down them. Anxiously I followed their course: would they crash or not, would they burst into flames or not, would they be blown up or survive?

"Faster!" she cried from below.

The sun was heating the streets without mercy. I fancied an ice cream in a little wafer tub, but I had to submit to her pace, or I'd be cast over the side of the ship which was sailing on without stopping – Mama never ate sweets.

We passed the Trade Union building, where a large sign said "Long Live the C.P.S.U.", then the dirty walls of the Inturist Hotel; we sailed down the former bed of the Poltva river, with us sailed Mickiewicz's column, the "Friendship" bookshop and a sign growing out of its rooftop torches that read "Forward to communism"; we merged into Lenin Avenue, and when we reached the Ethnographic Museum we collided with Klumba, the small square where unofficial protests were held. Strike, democracy, the Ukrainian language – I read the words torn from the newspaper headlines and now fixed to the trees with drawing pins, amid all of which the voices of elderly gentlemen were burbling away. Please don't let them recognise her, I thought to myself, but it was too late already – an old fellow in a cotton peaked cap with wisps of hair protruding on either side had taken her by the arm.

"Dear Miss Marianna," he rasped, "I believe there's a chance of free elections. You are our candidate for the U.S.S.R. Supreme Soviet."

She gazed at the old man benignly, her green eyes with golden glints shone for him, and she let the stream of her dearly loved voice flow for him, while at the same time gently freeing her elbow from the grip of his sallow fingers. We walked away, he stayed put, seeing us off with a fixed, goat-like stare, and I felt a sort of fleeting sympathy for him.

So what if a river once ran this way, if none of the sun-baked stones remembers it anymore, so what if according to legend fishing boats once scurried along the waters of the Poltva all the way to the Baltic? I took my mermaid by the arm, doing my best to keep up with her; we were almost the same height, and our shadows ran ahead of us until suddenly the shadow of Lenin, ringed by rose-bushes, devoured them. I looked at the five disconnected letters of his name and thought they could be written in a different way – if only, like a calligraphic design, a solid line were formed, with two passenger trains driving along it. Le-nin. Ni-nel.

"Faster!"

We came around the theatre from the left, climbed the steps to the stage door, and it closed behind us with its tangle of wrought-iron adornments; a sheaf of sunbeams caught between the metal flourishes. The doorkeeper ladies had spread their bulky bodies on some uncomfortable chairs, with the folds of their dark-blue coveralls spilling over the edges to shield an open bottle of vodka under the table. They handed Mama a set of keys and I made for the stairs, but Mama beckoned me to follow her – and I remembered that in March the director had thrown her out of her usual dressing room; she'd been transferred to the basement, and now she had the practice room of the recently deceased percussion player at her disposal. We walked down a long, windowless corridor, past a row of identical white doors, behind each of which different instruments were playing, though all I could hear was percussion.

Once in the room, she tossed her handbag onto a chair, lit a cigarette, and ticked off today's performance on a rota posted on the wall. I found a book in a grey cover lying on a locker, and opened it at random. "At the start of the twentieth century four men reigned on the world opera stage – Caruso, Battistini, Chaliapin and Titta Ruffo. And only one woman succeeded in rising to their heights – Solomiya Krushelnytska. Yet when it comes to personality, she by far outshone those famous men." Mama was flicking ash straight onto the carpet – she never appeared upstairs with a cigarette. She fetched Carmen's dress edged with dingy, tattered lace out of the wardrobe. By contrast, the red skirt that I was wearing was very new.

"It suits you," Mama said. "You can take anything you fancy from my wardrobe. You've grown up."

I peeped into the open door of her costume wardrobe; inside, as in our one at home, there was a hidden mirror, which reflected a long body like the ones I had seen in botany textbooks: a tree with a column-shaped part above ground, the apples of breasts, the speckled stems of arms and the leafy stems of legs, with the pollinium of an orchid between them.

"Zip me up," she said, presenting her back. "I'm tired," she whispered, more to the mirror than to me. "The norms for opera singers are absurd. Twenty-four shows a month, plus rehearsals. Every day! 'Milkmaid, strive for the highest yield from every dairy cow!'"

The only thing she said in Russian was the propaganda slogan at the end – the rest was in Ukrainian. One fine day, she had resolutely changed language – it was a bolt out of the blue for me and Aba. The quarrel, during which she had explained her reasoning, had been her final conversation in Russian, her native tongue. What she had said was that she was a daughter of this land, and this land was Ukrainian. She also said that Aba was an interloper, and that nobody had invited her here in 1944 – excuse me, but after the war you should have gone back to your Petersburg. She spoke of the Ukrainians who had fought for their city, Lviv, in 1918, and the desecrated graves of the Sich Riflemen. She spoke of the centuries-old burden of Russification and of the "Executed Renaissance" – Stalin's purge of Ukrainian writers and artists. She spoke of the incredibly low proportion of schools where native Ukrainians could study in their own language, and of the self-important invaders who have spent their whole life in this city without ever uttering a single word in Ukrainian. She mentioned the campaign that succeeded in eliminating many ethnically Ukrainian words from the dictionaries to make the language more and more like Russian, with the ultimate aim of having it blend with its "older brother".

Aba had reacted to this with an account of Polish Lwów and its numerous ethnic minorities, who lived together in harmony. She spoke of the Poles who fought for Lwów in 1918, and of the desecrated Eaglets' Cemetery. She spoke of the hospital where she had worked for thirty years, where each member of staff talked in his own language, which meant Russian, Ukrainian or Polish, and it never entered anyone's head to change it for ideological reasons. She also mentioned the Polish lullabies and the Russian primer, and she brought up the poets of the Russian Silver Age, whom they both loved so much.

Everything that Aba said passed without comment. As for me, I immediately understood and fully supported Mama's decision. Even

179

so, from the moment she changed language, I started to avoid talking to her – as if I myself had changed into a dictionary from which someone had excluded some of the words.

Now too I gave no reply, but intending to visit the ballerinas whom I knew, I went into the corridor.

And there gliding towards me were three dragoons in white silk waistcoats, holding three-cornered hats, with long feathers trailing on the ground behind them; the dragoons cackled, one of them began to reel and almost fell over; his eyes were filled with dirty mist. I walked after them, unable to remember exactly where the exit was, and together we skated forwards down the semi-circular tunnel, past the fire safety instructions, the evacuation plan, and a poster saying "Artists! Remember you are a son of Soviet soil", to a point where the corridor suddenly ended: dimmed lamps, ashtrays on cast-iron stands, and a sign saying "No Entry". I derailed like the coaches in Ufa, and made an about-turn, but it was too late: their laid-back cigarettes sent smoke into my face, a flutter of sniggers was aimed at me and a faded rose somebody had forgotten flew into the air. I ran away down the empty corridor, once more flitted past the row of closed doors, and went through the only open one to hoodwink the dragoons, who had no thought of chasing me anyway. I found myself in a dark, cavernous space; I'd never been in here before. The walls were a weave of pipes and other ironwork, decorated with valves, spigots, and doors leading nowhere; I could hear muffled footsteps and voices overhead. I was underneath the stage, in other words four levels below the mirrored studio where the ballerinas exercised and which I'd been in such a hurry to reach a minute earlier. I could see a tall, angular box of unknown purpose, and a candlestick equal to me in height. I stopped at the edge of an open sewer hole with a ladder set against it.

In the ballet studio I liked to sit on the floor and watch the manoeuvres of the ballet shoes, as dingy and grey as the lace on Carmen's dress, and I liked to inspect the ballerinas' hard stomachs, which were almost fused with their backs, and had no room for a child.

"You're very much mistaken," one of them once said to another in my presence. "The theatre has no connection with the sewers. And if it ever had, they'd have bricked it up."

Now I had the chance to check it out in person, but I wasn't sure if I should – Mama would be starting to worry about me, I deluded myself, pulling up the legs of my absurd tights and returning to the corridor. There I ran into the dragoons again, on their way back from the smoking corner; this time the lapels of their silk waistcoats were dusted with ash and rose petals, and now all three of them were reeling – the spectators must never find out about that either. After the dragoons, Mama came flying with her face covered in white powder.

"I'm off to have my hair done – go to the buffet and buy yourself a cake!"

The red skirt had no pockets, so clutching the coins, I ran after her, catching my hand for fun against all the closed doors along the way, making them unfurl like the lacy tape on her skirt; she dashed up the stairs, and I don't know how it happened, but along the way I entered that same door again.

"The body of a twelve-year-old girl was found in the stinking sewers," Vlad Listyev would say on T.V. "Her mother, a famous opera singer, is on the verge of madness because she blames herself for the tragic accident."

"Fragile, this way up," said the message printed on the weird box standing next to the candlestick. And also: "Musical instrument. Harp number 969". I imagined a conveyor belt, with a thousand harps travelling along it, straight into the capable hands of Soviet workers; there must be a production line like that somewhere in Siberia, amid the permafrost.

"The famous opera singer's daughter was caught by the militia just as she was throwing an antique harp down an open sewer hole, an instrument on which Soviet soldiers played during their solemn entry into Lvov on September 17, 1939", they'd write in the papers afterwards.

They had two kinds of cake at the buffet: cupcakes with white cream on top, and little horns with white cream inside. A musician in a dinner jacket was dozing on the steps, holding a violin; his bow lay across his knees like a *kinzhal* that he had just used to commit suicide. "Act One beginners to the stage please!" I heard the voice of Natasha, the stage manager. Carmen would be coming on stage in Act One to sing the Habanera; would everyone remember that in Act Four she'd have to die?

There was a little sweet cream on my blouse as I sat down at Natasha's feet on a coiled cable, from which I could see all the actors, the conductor's hands and the bottomless black pit of the auditorium. Natasha had a screen in front of her and was giving orders through a microphone hooked up to her desk: "Attention please – we're starting!"

Could the members of the orchestra hear the river gurgling

beneath the theatre during the pauses in the score? Did its underground flow have any effect on the course of the performance and the fortunes of the actors?

"Oh yes, there is a passage," said Natasha. "I've been in the sewers underneath the theatre, with your mother."

The older Natasha became, the more beautiful she was. She had white skin, as if coated in gold leaf. She had long, narrow eyes, like the women in Egyptian papyruses. Her thick, yellow-and-white curls were piled on her head like a stack of cream horns. Today she was wearing a long black dress. What a pity the audience would never see her.

"Why didn't you become an actress?"

"I wanted to be more important than that. The stage manager is like the controller on the railways – everything depends on him."

"Why don't you have a husband and children?"

"The theatre is my whole life."

"What does it look like underneath the building?"

"Wait a moment," she said, as she shifted two levers on her desk and hastily lit a cigarette.

"It was pure madness," she whispered, "no preparation at all, no protective clothing, just two weak torches. After the evening performance – in other words at the riskiest time of day, when most of the city's residents have a bath and the water level rises dramatically."

"Who was there?" I asked, whispering too.

"Your mother, me and a young set designer."

"And what was it like?"

She didn't answer, but stared urgently at the screen – I knew she couldn't always talk while working. The stream of Carmen's voice flowed on stage, the currents flowed in the collecting sewer beneath the theatre, the image on the television screen dissolved, the figures of the actors disappeared, and hissing grey water came into view instead.

"Not again!" Natasha exclaimed. "That electrician! When are they finally going to sack that skiving layabout?"

A suspicious noise came from the stage, quite like a dog howling. It was audible in the background to Carmen's aria, and even sounded as if it were in the right key, though I knew I was no expert in that field. Moments later the actors reappeared on the screen.

"I need this fight to stop me from getting too complacent," said one of the actresses in Ukrainian. "I can feel fear, a lot of fire and energy inside me."

That night, the three of them went down the same passage beneath the stage that I discovered by accident later on; it was two years after a member of the audience had died during "Aida", and two weeks before "Carmen" – Mama's last opera. Earlier, in the substitute dressing room, a minor scene had taken place. After the show, Mykola had come down to wait for Mama to get changed and remove her make-up. For quite a while they hadn't had a chance for a quiet conversation, and for quite a while she hadn't been to see him at his studio; her political activities were consuming all her spare time. He was annoyed. Her unannounced visits and the ill-defined nature of their relationship were no longer enough for him. His anger had grown so much that not even hearing her voice could bring the expected catharsis. He had come for declarations and joint plans. When she sat down facing him, he asked if she loved him – she said nothing, and looked away. He asked if she would marry him – she didn't even twitch. Then he moved towards her and gripped her wrists. She flinched, but still said nothing. Surprised by his own behaviour, he looked into her ashen face and tightened his grip.

"Say 'I love you'."

She said it – quietly, without looking him in the eyes – and at that point he realised this wasn't what he wanted. He let go of her hands, went upstairs, and fetched Natasha. The three of them drank a small bottle of vodka and decided to investigate the underground passage.

The sewer under the theatre was in good condition: it had high, semi-circular vaults and wide walkways that only narrowed occasionally, where the ceiling dropped. At one time, the collecting sewer had been linked with the cellars of the houses, and there were square concrete access points on the walls – they found them by touch as they groped for support and ran their fingers across the blind openings. It was slippery underfoot, and they were tripping over rats; Marianna walked in front, imposing her pace on the others. She had an old-fashioned lantern and was holding it high; whenever her arm tired, she lowered it for a while, and the billowing folds of her dress muted the small point of light.

They turned off the wide path, and walked bent double. The passage became very narrow, which alarmed them, so they back-tracked to the wide "street" and turned into another branch.

Now Mykola was in front, holding a torch, Natasha was behind him and Marianna was bringing up the rear, with her lantern. The water was rising higher and higher, and their voices and thoughts were drowned by the roar of the river as they walked on. The tunnel led up and up, then they passed a large weir, at which point another tunnel appeared to the right, and they found themselves close to the watershed.

They all came to their senses and began to regret that they'd got themselves into this adventure.

"I think we're under my house!" Marianna said, moving her face closer to the other two, so that they could hear her. And then Mykola raised his torch higher – as a set designer he must have known about lighting too – and, in full view of Marianna, he kissed Natasha on the lips. Marianna recoiled. Natasha responded to his kiss. They turned around and silently began to go back towards the theatre. On the way, Mykola stopped a few more times, raised the torch and kissed the beautiful stage manager.

I reached the same place – the point where the underside of our house was visible – and the thought of it gave me wings, as if suddenly I believed I could penetrate walls, rise like a wave over concrete, wood and glass, in seconds I could cling to Aba's warm, flabby stomach as she slept in her bed several storeys above us. The woman walking ahead of me turned and showed me stone steps leading upwards; willingly I began to climb them, worried only that the manhole through which we would emerge might be too close to the militia post – the men in uniform lurking there might nab us as soon as we came out and lock us in one of their gloomy cells.

I've ripped your black jacquard tights to shreds, Mama, I've dirtied your miniskirt, but the cold staircase refused to end, it led us higher and higher, I was getting out of breath, the scene around me was lighter and warmer, the steps were no longer of stone, but wood, still steep, tiring, tiring, tiring for tiny little feet of a size no bigger than thirty-three. Such were the feet of the female midgets flitting about the wooden steps, dressed in blue smocks and holding trays with food and drinks; now and then one of them dropped her tray and went flying headlong after the plates. Yes, here it was brighter than underground, but the light was faint and dim, and the air was stuffy, imbued with the stench of stale oil in which something had been fried. We were inside a long and narrow house, with only the space for a single room on each floor: a little booth on the ground floor, a library on the first, and on all the rest a café had been set up, where tall people sat at the tables and very small ones served them. One of the midgets, whose face was as strangely long and narrow as the house, had particular trouble delivering the orders: she tumbled on the stairs more often than the rest, injuring her knees – the blood was seeping through her jeans, and somehow I knew for sure that this very night she was going to die.

At last we reached the highest floor, and there stood a portly chimney sweep with the crumpled face of a clown, broadcasting like a radio – as he summarised the multicultural history of our city, his big fat fingers turned a brass button on his coat, and anyone who noticed that gesture understood that his words did not contain a single grain of truth. He didn't notice us as we blithely went past him, and followed a winding metal staircase to come out onto the roof.

Up there a warm wind tore the little hat from my companion's head, and briefly I thought I could see a black-and-white image of her subtle face, but the soil of the night sky was already being pierced by the lilac shoots of dawn. We were at the heart of the city, surrounded by the triangular Bernardine church, the rectangular

Town Hall, and the semicircular Dominican cathedral; flocks of white gulls were soaring over the roofs, as if we were by the sea. I got into a white open-top car parked at the edge of the roof, ready to travel onwards, but the woman's firm gesture stopped me.

At last I could take a close look at her. She was of a larger build than Mama, and as majestic as her own statue; she too was wearing Carmen's red dress, trimmed with snow-white lacy ribbon. Her hands were feeble, fragile and sickly, I knew they wouldn't support me if I started to roll down the sloping roof.

"Galicia, fickle Galicia," she said, without looking at me, and her round eyes were full of rage. "They jeer at me for singing in Italian. They criticise me for having an unschooled voice. They brought dogs to the Opera to imitate my singing by howling."

Each of her words seemed stamped in gold, as I sat down on the slippery roof tiles, terrified that something might interrupt her monologue.

"But I made a decision: I shall hold out to the last! I must convince all our pessimists that the Ukrainian soul too is capable of achieving the highest summits of art."

My gaze shifted down to her abdomen wrapped in red cloth, with the polygonal Jesuit church rising behind it.

"And what about love?" I asked softly.

"Music truly moves me. It's strange, because I'm cold-blooded and my nerves are as strong as steel. On stage I was hugged and kissed," she added. "Those were prearranged signs, signals to say they should raise the curtain or light the lamps. Everyone thought I was highly experienced, crafty even, but I was naïve. I kept passion at a distance. You see how strange an actress' life can be."

I watched with emotion as her body turned transparent; through her I could see a grey strip of sea on the horizon.

"Shall we go there, Solomiya?" I begged her, but she didn't answer. I got up, straightened my legs, and felt I must run to the lavatory. I started to go downstairs, asking the midgets for the toilet on the way; each one pointed in a different direction, but meanwhile my bladder was swelling, any moment now it would no longer withstand the pressure and would spill its contents. Finally, at ground level, I found a cubicle with a concrete floor. I locked myself in, nudged my head against some drying sheets, and the moment I lifted my skirt I saw a mocking, ugly male face squinting at my lower parts and cackling – it was baring its teeth at me from a television screen fixed to the door and shouting: "I can see! I can see everything!"

"Act Three beginners to the stage, please! Carmen, girls! Escamillo!"

It was Natasha shouting – I woke up at her feet, where I was sitting cross-legged on the coiled cable.

Then came Act Four with its famous, premeditated death.

After the performance, Mama and I walked home along dark, deserted Lenin Avenue. I was carrying a bouquet of white roses; she called the dark red ones "beetroots" and always left them at the theatre.

"When will they let you back into your old dressing room?" I asked, with a note of grievance that gave me a surprise.

"I don't think they ever will," she replied, in an even more unlikely tone because it was relaxed and sensual, and that's not how you talk to children. Then, to the rhythm of our weary steps, she made a sort of speech, of which I was afraid to drop a single word.

"I have devoted my life to art. Music is the only thing that truly moves me, so I've given it my all – I do nothing by halves. Men? I've had a few relationships, none of them was any good. Motherhood? I've never had enough time for it, but I do try hard to make sure of one thing: I've tried to instil some principles in you. So you'd know the difference between good and bad, so you'd never compromise with your own conscience, so you wouldn't tolerate betrayal under any guise. People think that lately I'm being persecuted because of my views, and that's why I'm losing my position at the theatre. And it's true, I won't be given new roles, I've been forced into the basement, and other nasty things have been happening – I am being persecuted. But there's something else too. My singing's worsening all the time, and some people know it. I've lost my motivation for the thing that had become my only purpose. But why? When I learned the truth about the Soviet system, my whole world collapsed. I felt I must fight against that system, but for ages I had no idea how. Now I have. People need me. Not the ones at the theatre, but the people in the street. I wonder if there's time for the theatre now. Singing for the chosen few, for the connoisseurs? Aren't art and the fight mutually exclusive? Shouldn't I devote myself fully to just one of them? I don't know. I've started to lose my voice. Maybe later, when we've defeated the empire and built a new, free country once again, I'll be able to . . . "

Without her finishing the sentence, we stopped at a bench. I looked to see what could have distracted her attention, but there was nothing curious happening around us, just a summer breeze caressing the ice-cream wrappers that someone had tossed on the ground.

Days after this, the shot rang out, and I forgot about that conversation for a long time. Later, when it suddenly surfaced from the depths of my memory, I wasn't sure if it had really taken place, or if I had made it up myself to suit my own theories, as fluid as water.

Russian Dolls

Great-Granma died at the age of ninety. All her life she had avoided everything to do with death: she steered clear of sick people, never went to funerals and grew angry if the topic wove its way into a conversation. Death took her by surprise, just when she had finally managed to forget about it. Unlike other old people, she had made no advance preparations for it, and all her days were exactly the same: she toddled to the shops, watched television, said her prayers, used her chamber pot and showered bile on her elderly daughter. One day – Aba and I were in the kitchen at the time – there was a mighty thump from behind her bedroom door; she had fainted and fallen over, hitting the back of her head on the floor. She'd been standing by the white linen chest which, as I later discovered, had played an important role in her life. The paramedics confirmed a stroke, and declared that "there's no point in taking her to hospital". I remember thinking that "there's no point" sounded like a handyman making a decision about a broken appliance. It occurred to me that now the entire system, which for decades had had its tasks and functions and altogether did a pretty good job, all the elements she had in mind when she said "me" – the muscles and arteries, blood vessels and eyeballs, hair and skin – had in an instant been seen as a thing, or as several different things, that nobody regarded as having any point or value anymore.

During the several days that she spent in a coma, I would drop into her bedroom, open the curtains and play the piano a little: I knew she was the only person who'd have regarded that cacophony as music. I'd raise her eyelids and study her eyeballs, that pair of rubbery, wet suckerfish, which from now on weren't worth much, like the balls for a game, such as snooker.

The day she died was laundry day. We laundered once a month, always starting at six in the morning, for lack of hot water in the taps after nine; we had a semi-automatic washing machine, and the rinsing was done by hand. At about eight, in a break between the sheets and a bedspread, Aba looked in on Great-Granma, and when she came back I realised what had happened because of the solemn look hanging from the frame of her glasses like a black ribbon. For a while we gazed at each other in silence, and then she said: "Let's finish the laundry first. We've only an hour left."

Not until the bed-linen and towels were hanging on lines in the bathroom and the water had gurgled its way out of the taps, did we start to deal with this and that. Over the next three days, while Great-Granma lay dead in her room, I did not go in to see her again. Each night Aba said the rosary by the corpse and lit a votive candle.

Some time afterwards, I discovered that the white linen chest standing to the left of the piano had featured notably in Great-Granma's love life. Even later on it came to light that my great-grandmother

Stanisława and my mother Marianna were very much alike, with one fundamental difference: Stanisława had once been madly in love.

Not with her much older husband, who had indeed adored her and carried her in his arms, despite which she had regularly thrown him out of the house – she would talk about it in old age too, explaining that a woman should know how to "stand up" to a man. On the day he was arrested, he had just come home after several days of banishment; they had spent the afternoon on a conciliatory walk with their daughter, but that night *they* had come, and he had had to go to the place of no return. Nor was she in love with the engineer who became her lover when the war started, and whom she followed to Kazan, along with his wife, of course. The wife regularly came to the flat where Stanisława and her daughter occupied a single room, she'd stand in the doorway and shout out all the epithets she knew in the Russian language to define a fallen woman. She wasn't in love with the handsome, unusually musically gifted Major Pavlov either, who towards the end of the war had taken her away from Kazan, and thanks to whom the whole family had ended up in Lwów. No. She had fallen in love with a German youth called Hermann, the only man in her life to have no connection with music.

For Stanisława, the post-war world in newly Soviet Lvov had colours, and best of all her favourite colour, green. Not yet thirty-five, she was a widow with a child, she smoked roll-ups made with cheap tobacco, she liked her extremely emaciated body the colour of opal and her large matt eyes the same shade as jadeite, and she worked as a secretary at the newly established district council, hastily set up in the former Regional Palace. In the spring she could weep with emotion as she stroked the bushes and trees: after work she would stop in a little square, she'd caress the fresh shoots of chestnut growing in the courtyard of their house on Pańska Street, soon to be renamed Ivan Franko Street: incidentally, she had far more affection for plants than for her own, then teenage, daughter. She wore a green linen dress that came as a gift from one of her former men, and always pinned one of her three brooches to the collar: a dragonfly, a butterfly or a pine cone.

On the day when she first saw Hermann, it was the pine cone – a delicately sculpted oval, willow-green in colour. He was about twenty, a platinum blond and a prisoner-of-war, who with some of his fellow-countrymen was working as a labourer for the city while waiting to go back to his *Heimat*. He knew rudimentary Russian, thanks to which he had become the mediator between the group of prisoners and the local authorities, and that was also the reason why he had come to the district council on some matter. He rarely smiled, but when he did, the gap showed between his top front teeth. At first sight, Stanisława knew that he aroused a strong desire in her, and the uncritical delight of a mother towards her child (a feeling which her own daughter was never able to stir in her).

Hermann was guarded less closely than the others, so he started to slip out of the barracks in the evenings and spend his nights at the flat on Pańska Street.

For the first time in her life Stanisława didn't bother trying to "stand up" to a man. She was shaken by strong emotions: a message to say that her lover couldn't come one evening would cause her several hours of compulsive weeping. Whenever they slept together, she woke up to look at him, and abandoned herself to passion-fuelled fantasies: she imagined that Hermann, as a former Wehrmacht soldier, would be condemned to death, and she would fall at the judges' feet and beg them to execute her instead of him. The alarm clock would ring at five, Hermann would get up in a bad mood, feeling underslept, and through the thin partition her daughter would awake; there was no room for her in Stanisława's fantasies.

The young lover was guarded in his behaviour towards Stanisława: he was happy to eat what she fed him, to bathe in the water she heated for him, and to penetrate the body she offered him. But as for her daughter, he fostered an irrational dislike of her – perhaps it irked him that she was a witness to their love affair. One fateful evening, the affair and the dislike both reached their climax.

That day Aba had a visitor: the upstairs neighbour, a lonely and eccentric widow. The two of them had agreed that she would obtain some paper and pastels, and Aba would paint her portrait. After a couple of hours, Hermann came by: the neighbour was wrapped in the coverlet from their bed, and was sitting on their pillows, with various props scattered around her – trays, bottles and vegetables; worse yet, both she and Aba were smoking cigarettes! This brash behaviour clearly upset the young German: he snapped a hostile remark and shut himself in the kitchen. In a chilly tone, Stanisława asked her daughter to tidy up, and then she went after him. Soon from behind the kitchen door they heard the thud of objects being thrown to the floor and stifled moans.

"It's not the first time," Aba impulsively told the neighbour. "Recently, Mama had a black eye."

"I'm going to inform the militia!" the neighbour shrieked, and dashed downstairs.

Aba felt the back of her neck turn to ice: a memory surfaced from

1937, the spectre of arrest, trains, camps, Siberia. Soon the militiamen appeared, banged on the door and shouted: "Open up!"

"Coming, coming," Stanisława called tunefully, having hastily changed into a dressing gown to pretend she'd just got out of bed.

The militiamen asked a few questions and set about searching the flat – meanwhile Stanisława's opal face took on a blueish glow, and her daughter kept a tight grip on her cheeks to stop her teeth from chattering. Luckily, it never occurred to the militiamen to look in the linen chest, where Hermann was hiding.

Following this incident, he started to come by less often, and soon after he went back to Germany. The three of them went on a farewell walk about the Kaiserwald woods at night, during which Stanisława told her daughter to walk a few metres behind them and to close her eyes when they kissed. I think she took her daughter with her purely to have a shoulder to fall on while walking home. The sharp metal feelers of the butterfly brooch caught on the hand-knitted sweater of the then teenage Aba, yanking out pieces of yarn, but the girl imagined it was Hermann's snout, and the visible gap between his front teeth, rushing after them and biting her on the shoulder.

And then . . . The fact is that Hermann didn't have to write that letter. Surely it couldn't have done him any harm to remain Stanisława's happiest memory?

The letter came three months later, written in Russian, but in the Roman alphabet, in that specific Volapuk which he had used in Lvov. In it he called Stanisława an "old ape", a "bitch" and a "hag", and said he had only come to see her to get warm and have a proper wash. Now unreachable in his *Heimat* behind the rising Iron Curtain, he quite gratuitously reviled her, her daughter, her city and her country.

In floods of tears, over and over again she read those remarkable, incorrect, patched-together words that might have been funny if not for their tragic content. Her daughter sat at her feet and stroked her hands. That was when the first hysterics had occurred, and the associated rituals. After the fiasco of her one and only love, Stanisława's character went to the dogs for good and all.

It must have been several days after the funeral when we set about tidying up. I remember how after dumping the heavy green drapes in the dustbin it turned out that between twelve and one in the afternoon a sunny yellow rectangle fell into Great-Granma's room and lay beneath the window like a steaming gold ingot. The smooth, ice-cold handles on the drawers of the linen chest also turned out to be the colour of gold. I remember how I pulled on each of them in turn, opened the drawers and didn't slide any of them shut again. Right on top lay her valuables, wrapped in yellowed paper: silver chains, rings and brooches.

"The jewellery will have to go to the antique shop – who'd want to wear such old-fashioned things now?" Aba said. For cleaning she'd pinned her curls on top of her head, and something about her exposed face was reminiscent of the fact that once she had been a little girl.

The rest of the drawers were full of documents and photographs, which she stacked in piles on the floor, bending over them anxiously, as if trying to use her shadow to shield them from my curious gaze.

I opened the little doors in the big ochre-coloured wardrobe, to let it effortlessly give birth to the clothes that hadn't survived the onslaught of moths. Overcoats, sheepskins and dresses fell to the floor with a crackle – they'd been sprinkled with dried orange peel. The clothes were to go "to the poor" – Aba didn't keep a single piece of frippery for herself.

Our cutlery, dark and heavy, glared with reproach at our attempts to co-opt into its company the lightweight aluminium spoons and forks we found on Great-Granma's table. Eventually they landed in the waste basket, followed by the piece of faded oilcloth on which they had lain for many years. Nor did we want the half-litre jar with a white deposit from which Great-Granma used to drink sweetened boiling water. Scoured to a shine, the enamel chamber pot had been stored beneath an emerald-covered sofa since the dawn of time: only days ago the ship of a body had rippled its surface, but now it was flat calm, with not a wavelet in sight.

We worked away for ages: first the yellow rectangle under the window grew lengthwise, and then it shifted to the courtyard wall. The colour of the bricks protruding here and there from its uncombed surface reminded me of the hair of the great-grandfather whom I'd never known.

We shifted the piano away from the wall and removed the dark sheets of cobwebs from it. I dragged some booklets out of a corner, sat down on the floor and started looking through them. They were pre-war, perhaps pre-revolution, with letters long since abolished from the Cyrillic alphabet, and they also included musical scores.

"What's this?" I asked. "Are these things Mama's?"

"No, they're her librettos," Aba replied reluctantly, looking aside, as she always did when her words were concealing something she couldn't say. According to an unwritten agreement in force between us we referred to Great-Granma as "her" and to Mama as "mama".

"She wanted to be an opera singer," Aba continued. "She had perfect pitch, a superb mezzo-soprano voice . . . "

I listened in amazement: why on earth was she announcing these well-known facts?

"I think it was from her that your mama inherited the timbre of her voice. In St Petersburg, she studied with Natalia Preobrazhenskaya – that name should mean something to you. But unfortunately she never sang in the theatre. She never got even the most minor role. She was too small, and as you know, height is enormously important on stage."

Great-Granma as an opera singer? I couldn't believe my own ears.

I gazed through the window at the illuminated wall outside – it was a theatrical stage, on which I tried to imagine Great-Granma. I put her in a red-and-black dress, crowned her with a shining diadem, and decorated her fingers with the rings from her drawers, but all in vain, because instead of Carmen's or Amneris' costume, I saw her faded dressing gown, shuffling slippers and wrinkled thumb as it felt the side of the kettle to see if the water in it were still warm. Following in her wake, I saw the stage at the Opera, with my own mother standing on it. Then I placed Great-Granma next to her and forced them to sing a duet – grandmother and granddaughter, old and young, small and tall. One had succeeded, the other had not, both were dead. The successful one had died young; the unsuccessful one had carried her failure for many decades.

"After being refused at the theatre, she joined the choir, and met your great-grandfather at rehearsals."

"But then he was arrested and the war began?"

"The worst time of all was in Kazan: she never said a word and constantly grew thinner – it was very hard to watch. She went to work at a factory. She hated that job, but it guaranteed us a bigger bread ration. She gave me her share, because I was growing and I was always hungry. Then Alexei Pavlov's choir came for a guest performance. And when it left Kazan, she went with it."

"But what about you?" I asked in horror.

"She couldn't have done otherwise," replied Aba with a note of resignation. "Singing was her entire life."

The bricks changed shape, first becoming black bread crusts, and then the bare walls of station buildings.

"Mama, *mamochka*, don't desert me!" cried Aba, running after the train, which was speeding faster and faster; her cry turned into a wail, deep and wild, very different from the sounds that her mother was emitting at the time.

In his photograph, Alexei Pavlov, the conductor, a dashing, handsome major, was looking straight at the camera. Goodbye, hated factory, goodbye, other people's connecting room! On the train, the new soloist was issued with an army uniform, and her first rehearsal took place in Pavlov's locked compartment, where he forced her to produce such high notes that they drowned out her daughter's farewell howling.

With Pavlov, she "stood up for herself" from the start: she became the lead soloist in the choir, and at night she performed her favourite operatic arias for him alone, taking note from the corner of her eye of the level of worship in his gaze. Summer and winter came and went, cities and concerts succeeded one another, until finally she landed in Lwów, a city as refined as Pavlov's new lady companion. The major instantly decided that they would settle here – he disregarded the rumours about dangerous Ukrainian nationalists preying on Soviets in the vicinity, and forgot about the librarian wife waiting for him in Moscow.

"Life in Kazan was sad and hungry. I lodged with our form mistress. What a joy it was when Mama wrote to say she wanted me to come and join her in Lwów!"

The little flat in Lwów was cramped, but right in the city centre. Pavlov had found one where none of the previous residents' furniture had been left behind – he abhorred looting, and they didn't mind having to sleep on the floor at first. A few days after Aba's arrival from Kazan, Pavlov had to go away on a brief trip with the choir, but then came the news that he had been killed by a stray bullet somewhere in Volhynia. Great-Granma began to smoke cigarettes and grew even thinner, her cheeks and eyes sank deep inside her body – down where her voice lived. Then came victory, the chestnut trees flowered, and Hermann appeared.

It was true: she never sang for him. She felt that the outburst of emotion that had shaken her whole being to its foundations posed a threat to her singing, because love had settled into her body in the very same spot where her voice had once resided. In that period, it very rarely made its presence known, and only during passionate sexual acts did she suddenly feel as if her lover's weight were squashing something like an advanced pregnancy, though her stomach was flatter than those of the slenderest ballerinas.

After Hermann's letter, her voice came back from exile and began to play tricks on her, seeking a new outlet; she didn't know how to rein it in, and so it was here, in her ever more frequent fits of hysteria that she would scream, wail and whine appallingly, as well as moan in a deep bass, and screech at a high pitch like a madwoman. On better days, it told her to step up onto an improvised platform at home and to perform her favourite arias, with or without an audience. To save herself from this range of noises, Aba began to paint holy pictures, including the Jesus I knew, in his crown of thorns, with green hair, streams of blood and his mouth half-open, clearly showing a gap between his top front teeth. At the time, this Jesus–Hermann had thrown Stanisława off balance: she had screamed and stamped her feet, insisting that he be removed from her sight. In her old age she had unexpectedly hung him up in place of honour in her bedroom.

In the next box there were photographs of army officers.

Some had Stanisława standing beside them – looking straight at the camera, she was always wreathed in cigarette smoke, while each of her companions wore the same facial expression as Yuri Gagarin after his first space flight. For many a long year, Great-Granma worked at the district council, and spent her spare time helping the talented army men to project their voices free of charge, meaning those who could perform the male part of her favourite duets well. The spontaneous singing lessons took place at her flat. Aba would listen from behind the door.

"A portrait of Grandpa Alexander," I remarked.

It was many years after the war when Alexander Pabian dropped anchor on Great-Granma's shore. Born near Donetsk, he was the taciturn conductor of the Lvov garrison orchestra.

"Excuse me, sir, that's not the right key. How do you conduct that orchestra of yours?"

He impressed the widow with his meekness and his melancholy, which she mistook for poetic grief, and also with the fact that he was much younger than she was – she was starting to age, and didn't know how to accept that with dignity. I don't know if they ever had a joint picture taken, in which he had the opportunity to adopt a Gagarin-like expression – if they did, it must have been destroyed later on. Aba added his portrait to the pile of others, pressed it to her chest and took it off to her room, but definitely didn't put it in the black casket with the profile of Chopin on the lid. The band director started visiting Great-Granma in the days when Aba was in love with the Polish pianist.

"Mama, please may I go out this evening?"

"With that two-bit musician? Out of the question."

"But why, Mama, why?"

Cue bravura chords and floods of tears. Chopin hadn't the temperament of a rebel, he cried at night, he cried on the platform, and then on the train, and on arrival in the Recovered Territories, newly granted to Poland in exchange for its losses to the east – he cried because her mother hadn't let them marry. All Aba had left were the polonaises, the letters in the black casket and those tears marking the shining path to the West, inaccessible to her. And then her mother had hit upon the satanic idea of marrying her daughter off to her own young lover, who had a steady career and no plans to leave the country.

The wedding was held on a weekday, and was conducted by the last parish priest at the church of Saint Mary Magdalene. In their first photograph together, the bridal couple are standing in front of the main entrance to the Opera, framed so that Lenin's statue can't be seen. Alexander is in civilian dress: a tall hat, a heavy winter overcoat and trousers with very wide legs that were fashionable at the time. He looks as if he's been told to put on a theatrical costume, and judging by the look on his face, he was dragged into the picture by force. The spectre of depression was already hovering over him, and the spectre of incurable illness was already over his bride.

Although Stanisława herself had pushed her daughter into this marriage, from the moment Alexander crossed the threshold of her flat in the role of son-in-law, she hated him. For years living in the same house, she managed her hatred perfectly, settling it into every room, in the kitchen and the bathroom, growing it in the soil of every appliance, cooking it into every dish, and fitting it into every word she uttered. It was devastation on the scale of a nuclear explosion. Grandpa was always sad, and he died young. Aba developed a chronic illness. Mama wasn't born out of love, and so she perished.

"Mama, you've ruined my life."

Not a word of rebellion was ever spoken. The daughter did as her mother said, for which her mother despised her even more. And so it went on for years: the daughter's silence engendered the mother's disdain, and vice versa, the silence and the disdain grew into each other – they formed a stronger bond between mother and daughter to the end of their lives than the fact that one woman's body had emerged from the other's. But then the granddaughter was born, and she had made an attempt to break free of this uterine incarceration.

"Granma, I've applied for the voice faculty at the conservatory."

"Out of the question."

"Why not, Granma?"

"You've no talent. You'll spend your life in poverty."

"Granma, I'm determined to be a singer. I do have talent. Do you hear me?"

"I'm going to open the window and alert the whole street that my own granddaughter is torturing me. The militia will be here in an instant."

"I'll open the window for you myself. Shout! Shout as loud as you can! Right now!"

Mama didn't hesitate to say the words that mattered most.

Great-Granma had her final admirer in her retirement, long after her son-in-law's death. The lonely violin teacher made her healthy meals and took her on walks. She liked it when he played for her, and for the most trivial offences she would hit him in the face. Despite his requests, she refused to move in with him – she didn't want to "abandon the family". I remember the day of this decent fellow's funeral – Great-Granma didn't go to the cemetery, but waited for a friend to bring her something from the reception. It was summer; in black lace gloves and a hat with a veil she sat astride a chair, while I walked around her in nothing but a pair of pink knickers. At some point she said irritably: "You shameless creature! Take a look in the mirror, see how indecent you are! Those knickers are too tight – everything you have between your legs is on display!"

Then I went up to the mirror and realised that she was right, though it would never have occurred to me earlier.

I blew the dust off the librettos and arranged them in order of year of publication. No longer illuminated, the surface of the court-yard wall had become the sea, and I was a scuba diver, looking for pearls in it. My great-granma was an unsuccessful opera singer, my granma was an unsuccessful painter, my mother was a successful opera singer, I would be a successful painter, my daughter would be an unsuccessful opera singer or a successful painter, her daughter, depending what my daughter chose, would be either a successful opera singer or a successful painter, lack of success times lack of success equals success, like in mathematics. We are like Russian dolls, one in the belly of another, it's not entirely clear who is inside whom, all that's apparent is who is alive, and who is not, we are like Russian dolls transpierced by a single shot, but I used to think Great-Granma wasn't in this chain. She was an unsuccessful opera singer, so my grandmother is an unsuccessful painter, but my mother, although she was a prima donna, is now dead.

Aba came back for the rest of the papers – she wasn't capable of taking the entire pile away in one go.

"In her old age she sang in the Cathedral," I said.

"Very rarely, and only on weekdays. She had a friend in the Cathedral choir."

"*The ri-i-ighteous dwells in your holy hill.*
Who may abide in Your tabernacle,
Lord, who may dwell in your holy hill?
He who walks uprightly, he who works righteousness,
And speaks the truth in his heart,
The ri-i-i-ghteous dwells in yo-o-our . . ."

The Mass was said in the brightness of gold-rimmed lamps, but as usual, she was never invited on stage. Long before her death, she had a great deal of white, wrinkled skin, which coated her like a ragged shroud; perhaps at home, behind the locked door of her bedroom, she took it off, like the toad prince, and released from inside it the slender Cio-cio-san who performed her best arias, while we thought it was the television. We saw the white hair with the childish centre parting, the spectacles with thick lenses, and the elephantine legs covered by the dressing gown, as urine dribbled down them – drip-drip-drip – to made sure the source never ran dry, she'd toddle to the kitchen with her jar, put her thumb with its neatly filed finger-nail to the kettle, and pour out boiling water. She took care of her manicure to the very end.

Aba held a cloth in her swollen fingers and dusted the face of Jesus. For all these years He had seen Great-Granma slicing sausage on the oilcloth, chewing it laboriously with her remaining teeth, and lying down to watch black-and-white films, He had heard her farting loudly, sighing and humming songs. Did Jesus wait at night for her to switch off the television and, rubbing her bum against the creaking sofa springs, to sit down and row her outspread arms towards Him?

"In the name of the Father and the Son, Jesu, Jesu . . ."

Was He looking when the tears appeared on her cheeks, while she peered over her glasses to check if anyone had noticed?

"What a bad daughter, what a bad granddaughter, they never invite their mother to share their table!" she said – to me, or to Him? Did Jesus ever hear her maligning her old daughter in the kitchen?

"You idiot! You damned fool! You cow!"

"You're the fool," Aba would answer her, sounding disconcerted.

Her mother would bump her backside into her in the narrow kitchen passage, or even push her, and a stream of powdered plaster would trickle from a hole in the wall onto the crooked lino.

"You shameless whore!" she'd whisper, as she lay in wait for her granddaughter in the hall when she came home late from the theatre. "What doorways have you been lurking in?"

We were like Russian dolls, but only we three. There was no room in the chain for her, she was evil – nobody wept when she died.

Ever since the concierge had gone to prison, Luba had been cleaning our courtyard. In a dishevelled state, she went about with a broom and a shovel. She threw the rubbish down the dark sewage hole, into which the caretaker's children poured the contents of their bucket; she dropped the bodies of the pigeons she killed down there too. They were eaten by the monster living at the bottom, who also swallowed the last rays of sunshine that crept across the yard. Oh well, Great-Granma's bedroom faced north, and it was always rather dark in there.

"These brochures are worthless. We'll take them to the Opera purely as a historical curiosity," said Aba about the librettos, when she came back without the photos, which she'd finally managed to put away somewhere. "We'll make this room into a dining room," she continued. "We won't have to carry our food from the kitchen to the main room anymore, and that'll make it easier for us to keep the carpets clean."

The Polish–Ukrainian War

"I've got a headache, I think I'm about to have a migraine," I said in a low, childish voice, knowing how pathetic it sounded.

Mykola wasn't listening, or was pretending not to listen, as he strode towards Teatralna Street, where he had planned to make the first stop on our walk.

It was a sunny afternoon in June, but that summer I thought my streets had been deprived of shade and moisture, my streets were going dark and starting to accuse me by hanging out flags with black ribbons on a daily basis, and they were accusing him too, permanently wrapping him in a rainbow of seven shades of gloom, except that it didn't depress him in the least – on the contrary, he seemed to have grown, I didn't even reach his chin, he was rising upwards, as if he had wings, like Perseus, on his artist's sandals, and as if he also had them on the artist's bag that was always slung across his shoulder. I hauled myself after him, feeling sore, dragging my feet, crawling like a snake. It could all have been different if we had simply remained friends, I thought. If you two had persisted in purity, whispered the bright walls of the Cathedral, which we happened to be passing, and which I had started to avoid, because the ethereal Jesus inside was going black and his face looked charred.

"Clear and simple, like the blow of an axe," Mykola explained. "In just one day the city split in half."

I've heard this somewhere before, I thought, but I couldn't remember where and when.

"You're right," he said, though I hadn't spoken. "Its former integrity was just an illusion, and of course you know how pleasant it is to live in a fool's paradise."

We passed a school, and the eternally closed Dzieduszycki Natural History Museum, and went into the former Officers' Building.

"Don't look at the memorial plaque," he ordered, shielding my eyes with his hands like horse's blinkers. "It's not just ugly, it gives false information too."

Nobody stopped us in the cold vestibule, and we went up the stairs.

"This is the place where it all started. This was home to the National House, the main cultural headquarters of the Ruthenians of the day, who had an increasing sense of being Ukrainian. The special thing about this building is that it had three entrances from three different streets – Teatralna, Korniakt and Ormiańska. There's no spot from which one single person could have watched them all at once. That was the reason why Vitovsky chose this building as the seat of the Sich Riflemen's general staff – they were the Ukrainian army."

As I looked through the window, Mykola's figure replaced the silver knob of the Town Hall tower, with the Ukrainian flag flying above it; moments later it was the Town Hall itself that said to me: "It was no small challenge for Vitovsky's soldiers to find some large enough pieces of blue and yellow canvas to hang from the Town Hall the night before November 1. There was no such thing in Polish Lwów. At the last moment the day was saved by a caretaker at the 'Narodna Torhivla' – the first Ukrainian trade cooperative; he fetched out the banner they hung over their stall at major festivals. After the war it was kept in the museum, but later the Soviets destroyed it. It's exhibit number one in the imaginary collection that I want to show you today."

From the top of the tower, two sheets of brightly coloured fabric flowed down to the ground and drifted after us across Teatralna Street; I furtively tried them on Mykola, wrapping his body in them, I wanted to know if martyrdom suited him, but my fantasies foundered on his stern glare – he had no wish to share the memory of the corpse swathed in the Ukrainian flag. Other hands had unwrapped and kissed the familiar scar between the shoulder blades, another tongue had licked the dried blood from the freckled glades, other fingers had dressed the body and fitted it into the hard bed of the coffin.

"Vitovsky had machine-gun nests established at pivotal points in the city. Their barrels were aimed at the passers-by on Holy Spirit Square and on Hetman's Embankment, protruding from the balcony of the Opera, and from the terrace of the Viennese Café."

"Shooting from there is a local tradition," I joked, but neither of us smiled.

After all, there were other traditions – such as playing chess in the avenue leading to the Opera; we were just passing the little benches occupied by pensioners, good afternoon – good afternoon – if you please – I'm white, so I'll start – now it's black's move, I wonder who's going to win this game.

"November 1, 1918 was a tragic day for this city. The beginning of the end of it – as it had existed until then. And it doesn't matter how the war proceeded after that. It doesn't matter who was the victor and who was defeated."

"What's needed are two parallel cities with two different names, Lwów and Lviv – did anything like that come up at the time?" I asked.

"Two cities with the same Market Square, trams, and chestnut trees? But it was one single city, and that's why the war began that divided it in half anyway?"

The stocky Opera house fluttered on the smooth surface of gas-filled balloons growing in bunches held by salesmen along the avenue. They were part of a bad stage set, just as bad as the stage set for her funeral: flags, crowds, a band. Someone else had bestowed the final glance on her, someone else had closed the coffin.

"Watch out for the manhole covers," warned Mykola, as we rounded the theatre. "They're not always shut properly and it's easy to fall in."

Horodotska Street looked like a red-hot tunnel without a single small tree, as trams, cars and minibuses tried to thwart each other's plans on the obstacle course of its undulating cobbles; ignoring the traffic regulations, we stepped into the roadway, to be hooted at from all directions, but we just continued to roll along the tracks like two tramcars, or maybe like two trams linked by a tow rope.

"I'm not going to give you a tour of sites of glory in arms for either side. I'm not going to show you the heroic sites or symbols, I shall avoid the tired old phrases such as 'the defenders of Lwów'. I shan't say a word about the teenagers who were later called 'the Eaglets'.

But I'll show you a few things that were discarded or forgotten. Things that didn't fit into the legend."

After the unfortunate flag came the explosion that missed its target. As Mykola narrated, I imagined the whole scene: the Ukrainian lads lost amid the urban landscape that was alien to them, and the Polish lads who, despite being in their own city, failed to blow up the barracks, perhaps because in previous years they had been trained for something other than destroying buildings. There was sand everywhere, in their boots and in the air, in piles all around them, scattered along entire streets; it was as if the wind were just about to blow and a sandstorm would start, sending a mixture of dust and hot air overhead, above the trams, and above the cupola of Saint Anne's, the church that straddles Horodotska and Shevchenko Streets, which in Soviet days was a furniture store. It wasn't sand, but another, lighter substance that the Polish students poured into their pockets, before descending into the sewers, feeling at home in the entrails of their beloved city; under the ground, time and again they reached the Ferdinand barracks, the westernmost bridgehead of the Ukrainian front. They worked like ants, going to and fro with their pockets full, up and down. Although the enemy fired on them from the barracks, it never crossed their minds that at the very same time they were being approached from underneath, and that a large heap of dangerous powder was growing in the cellars by the day.

The entrails of their beloved city. The sewer beneath the theatre. The greatest humiliation in his life.

On the day of the action, the street shook to its foundations, but the Ferdinand barracks didn't so much as tremble. The Poles from what was then Bem Street had miscalculated the distance – the blast went off a few metres too far along.

"I love you" said under duress, "I love you" without any value, "I love you" said once and never again before death, after which nothing can be mended.

The men in the barracks were terrified of fire. The sight of rags soaked in paraffin, which came flying through the windows and started blazes here and there, sent them into a state of irrational panic. They had grown up in country cottages thatched in straw, and they didn't know that fire couldn't consume thick stone walls quite so easily. One of them was the poet Roman Kupchinsky. He was sitting alone in one of the rooms, when suddenly the door caught fire. In just a few seconds, the small tongues of flame became a burning wall, abruptly moving towards him. There wasn't any water to hand, but there was a pot of beetroot soup, so quick as lightning, Roman grabbed it. Bright red broth went gushing into the bright red jaws. And thus the bounty of the local countryside defeated the beast of war.

Things were different whenever the beast came to me in my dreams – I had no way to defend myself, for why should I? It didn't seem interested in me, but it wouldn't let me leave, I had to look at it. This was at the circus, but not the real one, on Horodotska Street, where the clowns' outsized yellow shoes raised dust and performing kitties in costumes danced in the arena, but in an unfamiliar one, set up in a former church – that was where the beast's solo performance took place: it danced without a safety rope right under the cupola, it juggled with ball lightning, it did acrobatic tricks before a yelling, cackling audience. I was chilled by the thought that I was taking part in the profanation of a temple, that I was watching as the brute ruled the roost in a place that belonged to the six-winged seraphim. I was turning to ice, more and more rapidly, till the moment came when the beast started swinging on the trapeze. Amid salvos of laughter it flew over the spectators' heads straight towards me, and once it was near enough to touch, it blew a bubble-gum balloon into my face.

After the collapse of the empire, the circus building on Horodotska Street began to disintegrate. The plaster started peeling off the façade in layers, and the paving tiles near the entrance crumbled, destroying the shape they had once been given, and forming bumps, potholes and uneven surfaces. Just as with people, whose faces in old age betray the whole truth about the choices they've made in life, here too the children's arcadia, stripped of the chance for further pretence, exposed all its heart-breaking ugliness. The face of her mother – the lame failed painter – Mykola had also run away from the funeral because he wanted to avoid looking at that face.

We passed the circus, and climbed a hill crowned by a grandiose Orthodox church.

"My next exhibit are letters," said Mykola. "While the Poles and the Ukrainians were killing one another, two archbishops were writing each other letters which a courier carried across the front line."

A red-and-white Polish flag flew above Saint George's Cathedral – the seat of the Ukrainian Greek Catholic church, headed by Metropolitan Archbishop Sheptytsky. "At Sheptytsky's place it's Poland, and at mine it's Ukraine," wrote the Polish Roman Catholic archbishop Józef Bilczewski. "May the fratricidal fighting end immediately, for the Day of Judgement awaits every one of us. During a search at my palace," Sheptytsky complained in his reply, "the Polish soldiers went through all my private correspondence." To which Bilczewski replied that he couldn't sleep, because Ukrainian bullets were coming in his windows; he suggested that this very Sunday each of the city's three archbishops, including the Armenian Catholic Teodorowicz, at his own cathedral should entrust the city and the country to the Sweetest Heart of the Lord Jesus, with a request to turn civil war and anarchy away from us. The distance between the two hills is not at all far – from Saint George's you can run down the hill in a flash, and then there's only a short uphill stretch to the palace at the foot of the High Castle. It was impossible to take a straight path – there were barricades and patrols everywhere, and they were shooting everywhere, so the courier ducked down side streets, through heaps of leaves that hadn't been cleared since the war began; it crossed his mind that instead of leaves he was treading on the letters that he carried throughout this war from one hill to the other, from Sheptytsky to Bilczewski and back again. Outside it was November, dusk fell early, and from the open doors of Saint Anne's came singing – *O Queen of Poland, pray for us* – but there was a smell of smoke, free Poland was nearer and further than ever before. On one hill, they whispered to him that Sheptytsky had a telephone behind the altar with a hotline to the Ukrainian front, and on the other they insisted that Bilczewski had had an electric bell installed in his bedroom with a direct connection to the clerical students' apartments. In previous years the city had been full of snow in November, but this year it wasn't; if it were to fall now, would they still go on killing each other, he wondered? The back streets were quiet; a fearless lamplighter rode past on a bicycle with a long metal pole to open the window panes and light the gas in the streetlamps,

217

but the courier's mind was on the letters that he was carrying in his inside coat pocket – he wouldn't dare to open them, not if a pistol were put to his head. He didn't want to know what was in them, as long as the archbishops continued to write to each other, as long as they continued to unfurl their prayers above the streets, prayers that carried him smoothly from one hill to the other and made him invisible to the soldiers on both sides of the front. "But what sort of barbarity is this? On the streets they've captured, the Ukrainians are blotting out the Polish inscriptions with mud and destroying the monuments," Bilczewski thundered to Sheptytsky, and now, in the 1990s, I noticed that the street names were once again obscured with white paint: the Soviet names had been removed, but new ones hadn't yet been invented.

"It looks as if that war never ended – it's still going on, isn't it?" I asked.

In reply Mykola smiled, and for the first time that day looked me in the eyes. At that moment the refrain of that French song crossed my mind, as the best expression of what was happening between us: *Je t'aime . . . moi non plus* – I love you . . . me neither.

From Horodotska, we turned into one of the side streets with an obliterated sign.

"This is where an unlucky grenade was thrown," he said.

Red apples irregularly shaped like cylinders or polygons, spotted with a mild rash, slightly nibbled by birds and maggots, perfect for preserves, the apples in a bowl on the windowsill held her glance for the last time in her life. Seconds ago she had run up to the window, because she'd heard a shot fired by the watchman from this house at an enemy patrol as it went past in the street. In response the

Ukrainians had instantly thrown a grenade, killing her on the spot; what had shortly before been her now fell to the floor, which was bursting into flames. Into the flat rushed Chersky, and threw himself flat on the scattered apples. "The Ukrainian cadet had accidentally killed his Polish fiancée," the papers later reported. How did he go on living after throwing that grenade? There's nothing written about that anywhere.

For the first three years after the fatal shot, Mykola lived in three connected freeze-frames: crushing Marianna's slender hands as he squeezed them, going under the ground, and gently entering Natasha's mouth.

We walked on towards Copernicus Street.

During the fighting, the Main Post Office changed hands several times, and when the Poles were inside it, with the Ukrainians blockading it from outside, one of the Poles devised a system involving a rope. A thin line was stretched high above the street, linking one of the Post Office windows with a nearby house on Kraszewski Street; a small box slowly travelled along it, carrying letters and food to the soldiers trapped in the Post Office. One of the Ukrainians made the box into a moving target and set up a shooting contest: if the Ukrainians hit it, pots of soup and main courses fell to the cobblestones. Then the Poles attached a bust of Taras Shevchenko to the box and the firing immediately ceased. Later a fire broke out and it was obvious to both sides that they had to abandon the building, to let the neutral firemen get inside.

Three years on, the fires of mourning and self-recrimination went out. Mykola let his hair grow, unleashed his career at the academy, and got married.

There were moments when that war had a human face. At sunset, arms were suspended and there was joint feasting. Ukrainian waiters guarded Polish dynamite, and vice versa, plenty of vodka was drunk and many photographs were taken, which didn't go into the patriotic albums: the Polish legend remained black-and-white, and the Ukrainians didn't create one of their own. At the Ferdinand barracks, a Polish–Ukrainian ball was held, during which drunken officers complained to each other of mass desertions and agreed on the positions they'd spare the following day.

"Did you know that this is where the Jewish district began?" asked Mykola, when we went back to Horodotska Street.

I shook my head in denial.

"The Jews played the role of a polygon that doesn't fit in. They made up a third of the city's residents, but the Poles and Ukrainians fought for it over their heads. Officially they were neutral – the militia they formed wore white armbands. But once the Poles had taken the city, they suspected the Jews of favouring the Ukrainians and carried out a pogrom."

We reached a decaying playground. I sat on a wobbly swing; the inscription on a memorial plaque fixed to the wall beside it told us there had once been a synagogue here, but someone had scratched off the six-pointed star with a sharp instrument. On the day when the fighting for Lwów ended, the streets where the Jews lived went up in flames, and so did the seventeenth-century Hasidim Shul Synagogue, adorned with a ceremonial Renaissance attic in the local style. The drape, or *parochet*, modelled on the decorative curtain that separated the Holy of Holies from the rest of the long since devastated temple in Jerusalem, had fallen, the cantor was singing, and the rabbi was entering the *bimah*, but the exalted podium began to shake and sway in all directions – in its place a merry-go-round was built, with slides and swings that left rusty marks on my clothing.

All Mykola's academic essays were on stained-glass windows, and the swan song was a widely discussed work about the stained-glass window from Marianna's stairwell. It was a form of therapy – as if the pieces of coloured glass that he saved from destruction had the power to heal his own wounds. And then a girl with her eyes and complexion had come out into the stairwell and briefly eclipsed the stained-glass window.

Copper coins jingled in the lap of the toothless conductress on tram number seven – there was a roll of tickets sticking out of her bag, and in reply to my announcement that I had no money she sniggered, because she was just like me – she couldn't care less how many tickets she sold today or tomorrow, she knew nothing depended on it; despite the fact that Mykola was trying to pay for me, she toddled off to the other end of the car in her battered carpet slippers, scrambled onto the conductor's platform and dozed off.

We reached the grassy open space below the entrance to the cemetery, where I sat down on the grass; the white of Mykola's shirt was whiter than the white crosses of the Polish Defenders of Lwów, brighter than the bright colonnade, the figure of Mykola was taller than the Archangel Michael's column, which had recently risen to the left of the Eaglets' graves, and his voice was softer than the swish of the dry grass.

"We are witnesses to the artificial inflation of the issue of reopening this cemetery. It's being steered by politicians on both sides of the border. They're deliberately reinforcing the divisions and the stereotypes, while acting the part of great patriots, and people believe them, because they're used to slogans and legends."

He paused, closed his eyes and lowered his voice even more. I felt as if the words he was about to utter would be in some way irreversible.

"Listen to me: there's proof that the bones are mixed up. There are Poles and Ukrainians lying side by side at the Eaglets' cemetery, and there are boys and girls from both sides of the front at the Sich Riflemen's burial site at Yanivsky cemetery too. 'We fought each other face to face, and now we're lying together, arm in arm.' During the fighting a military hospital was set up at the main Polytechnic building, and the wounded were taken there. The doctors tried to save everyone, regardless of ethnicity, or on which side they'd been fighting. Whenever someone died, they were buried nearby."

"But there were exhumations later on."

"Yes, after the war they sorted the bones and buried them in the various military cemeteries. But by then it was hard to do it precisely – the bones were already mixed up."

"We fought each other face to face," I repeated, thinking of Mama. She never saw the face of the man who shot at her from the roof.

Weakened by the secret confided in me and by my headache, I lay down on the grass. The migraines had first appeared when I started being with Mykola. Even Aba was helpless, though in the past she had saved me from mumps and chickenpox, lice and worms. Migraines can't be cured, her doctor friends tried to persuade her, but she wouldn't give in, and kept stuffing me with a variety of pills – they were all white, just different in size and shape, but none of them helped. Aba was surprised, but I wasn't in the least – to me the situation was as clear as day: the pain was the direct consequence of sin, in other words, an affair with a married man.

Mykola too tried curing me with little white pills – his were smaller, like granules. Just like Aba, he refused to admit that they might not work, and kept bringing me new varieties, tipping them into my mouth by the handful; while I, choking, would gibber that suffering was the outcome of sin, to which he would say yes, and then instantly massage my mouth with his hard tongue, also as a form of therapy. Aba poured scorn on his homeopathy, but I swallowed whatever they brought me; it was all the same to me.

We were both tired after following the Polish–Ukrainian battle trail. The sun had lit a bonfire in my head, the rising pain was smouldering away in there, gaining new ground by the millimetre, broadening the offensive, trying to conquer me entirely; I put up no resistance, I opened the gates to it, I was in a hurry to sign the act of capitulation. I collapsed into a clump of weeds, and took a lighted cigarette from Mykola. We were sitting in a meadow near the former Pioneers' Palace, yet another Soviet ruin, later renamed the Palace of Youth, although Palace of Euthanasia would have suited it better; the cigarette was finished, and yet grey powder kept landing on my top – it must have been plaster from the walls. Ashes, charred remains, graves in the streets, garden squares and courtyards – the usual residue of civil war, the fire was out, leaving streaks of smoke, but they too would disappear along with one last drag on the ciga-rette before tossing the butt into a dustbin. I turned to ask Mykola for another one, and saw that he'd fallen asleep: every part of his body was spread out on the grass separately – just as the findings from archaeological digs are exhibited, when each object has to be clearly visible from all sides.

I was sitting in a circle drawn on the grass by the ash from the packet of fags I'd smoked, watching Mykola as he opened his eyes and slowly stretched his bones.

"How do you combine it all?" I asked in a whisper. "The sculpting, the lectures, the history of the city?"

"You have to study intensively until the age of thirty. Then you just prove yourself in action."

My time until thirty seemed like an endless corridor with lots of half-open doors on either side – luckily it was long enough for the unsettling moment of "proving myself" to be well out of sight, somewhere in the distance. We walked towards the tram loop.

"And what would you do if a Polish–Ukrainian war broke out in Lviv today?" I asked.

"I'd put a bullet through my head," replied Mykola in a tone bristling with sincerity; with an imperious wave he hailed the number seven tram, which was scheduled to stop at the place we had reached anyway.

The Stained-Glass Window 2

The new building in the gap in the old block was known as "the filling", though if we had wanted to stick more precisely to the terminology of dentistry it should have been called "the denture". We were all certain that it wouldn't blend in here – in this company of high-born Austrian residential houses it was bound to be a bastard – so the long wait for its birth, which went on all spring, summer and part of the autumn was completely joyless. It started with a terrible din that took possession of our narrow little street – here and there concrete mixers whirled, and behind a hastily erected blue fence time and again, a long yellow crane bowed down, kowtowing to a false idol.

That spring, Mykola received an urgent commission, and we only saw each other in passing: a quick coffee in the daytime in dismal dives calling themselves cafés, and at night the lilac-scented grass of Stryisky Park, under-illuminated, under-cleaned, and quiet. We avoided my house because of Aba and her indignant glare, which concentrated all her disapproval of our relationship. We kept away from Mykola's studio, because he had decided that the new sculpture was going to be a surprise for me, and I would see only the finished work, in its full splendour.

Another reason why I was finding it hard to stay at home was that Aba had started to feel worse. The drugs that had brought her relief for the past few decades had now stopped working, and nothing new had been invented. All her joints hurt, the most painful being her ankles, knees and fingers. When her door was ajar, I would often hear her softly groaning with pain as she lay on the couch. She went to see her doctor friends for advice, but came home disconsolate – nobody knew what to do. Helplessness hung in the air. I had no idea how to restrain her illness as it worsened by the day, and she didn't know how to break off my affair, which she was convinced was destroying my life. Whereas I was convinced that what was happening to her was all my fault.

The street vibrated day and night. The cobblestones shook beneath the wheels of the construction machines, agitated drivers hooted on finding no way through, and the windowpanes in all the surrounding houses resonated. Compactors, road-rollers and vibratory rammers worked away. Drills shuddered. Pumps trembled. Concrete slabs fell with loud crashes. Clouds of dust hung in the air. Behind the closed window of the house next door, an old lady grappled with a stained compress crookedly tacked to her forehead. The labourers setting all these tremors in motion were not enjoying their work. They were old and poor, and they had a long journey home. Later on, when the walls of the bastard building began to rise from the ground and climb higher, they went up the scaffolding without any safety gear. One morning in July, one of them fell and was killed. He lay on the cobbles for hours – anyone so inclined had plenty of time to see the outline of an extra head, formed beside the shattered one by a pool of blood, and his extremely shabby boots coated in something resembling white school chalk. For our little side street, this building site was a major earthquake.

Whenever I asked Aba how she was feeling, she'd deign to give me a dry report. By now she always spoke to me in a way that made it clear she was angry with me. The fact that she had stripped me of her love was tearing me apart, but I knew I deserved it. I started responding coldly and rudely, doing my best to mock and insult her at every opportunity. We both avoided even the most trivial mention of Mykola, though he of course was setting the pace of life for each of us. That summer, I would come home very late, but she never went to bed until I was back, which drove me up the wall. Requesting, shouting and having a row were no use at all – she'd always wait to the bitter end. She'd be sitting in front of the television, or saying the rosary in Great-Granma's old room, or nodding off on the sofa in the main room. Or she'd be lurking among the flowers on the balcony. When I finally crept into the flat – moistened by kisses, electrified by caresses, set on fire by orgasms – she'd cast an ominous glance at me without a word and finally go to her room, after which neither of us could sleep anyway. I remember one of the hottest nights of that July. Mykola and I took a long time to come back from the other side of the city, and then spent just as long under my balcony. It was already so late that soon it would be early morning; there were no lights on in any of the windows, and we were hiding in my little street as if inside a giant Coca-Cola can after licking the last of the sickly-sweet drink from its walls; now the can was pounding to our movements, half undressed we were reaching a climax standing up, and the old wooden gate was squealing to our rhythm. And then I saw her watching us from the balcony. In a swarm of curlers, her head was protruding from among the flower-pots, and the shining lenses of her spectacles were trained on us. We were standing under the only lamp in the entire street, and it was on. I felt shame and fury, and from that moment on, I stopped talking to her.

In that period, Mykola was educating me on relief sculpture, so we were studying the memorial plaques that had sprouted in the city centre like mushrooms after rain, or rather toadstools after Chernobyl. Valery Bortiakov from the Polish theatre had thought up the term "sculpting in bars of soap", which had caught on in their circle. Whenever they tried tracing the provenance of the individual plaques, it always proved quite simple: anyone who had some money and an idea could go to the city council and obtain permission. If the person they wanted to commemorate was politically correct, the officials granted it, and washed their hands of the matter. The applicants could choose their own design and sculptor. From time to time, the municipality sponsored a plaque, and then at least the initiator's name was known. In this way, a succession of works had appeared that caused real artists to clutch their heads in despair at first sight. Or to avert their gaze as they walked along the street.

As we wandered the city, we found that most of the plaques were too large, hung too low and broke the rules of composition, but above all they clashed with their surroundings. Aliens from another planet compared with the churches and houses, they were growing on the old buildings like mould. Here five egg-shaped heads stuck out of the wall, all crammed into a single oval. Over there some bronze shoes were jutting out – any passer-by might catch his head against them. Elsewhere the face of a cretinous doll stared with goggle-eyes.

Usually we didn't recognise the person whom they commemorated; worse yet, we didn't want to know who they were – Ukrainian history lost out against good taste. We'd discuss one, and the next day three more would appear. We'd talk about another, and the next day it would be gone without trace – vagrants stole them for scrap metal.

Mykola reckoned the Soviet plaques were better. Not all of them, but still. I found this idea astonishing: it brought unbearable confusion into my thinking about the world. It proved the impossible extent of its ambiguity.

"In those days, the city was grey and neglected, but it kept its personality. Today's surgical experiments on its body are going to transform it into something else."

When Mykola uttered these words, which stuck in my memory, we were on the corner of Copernicus and Słowacki Streets, where not long ago, a robotic figure in a military cap had been embossed. Afterwards as he walked me home along Stefanyk Street, he explained the differences between high, low and hollow relief. As we entered my gateway, he started to kiss me. Meanwhile I stared at the little round window carved above the front door to avoid seeing the cracks in the walls. I was pretending to myself that they didn't exist.

In that period, I made up myths about them – imagining they were the webs of large spiders that Luba had missed while cleaning, or the decorative fluting we'd been told about in art history class, or distortions caused by the contact lenses I never wore. When the first cracks appeared in the walls and ceiling, Mykola documented them by borrowing a piece of artist's charcoal from Aba, putting a date by each one, and taking photos. The neighbours took no part in this: the people upstairs were getting ready to emigrate to Germany, and a while ago something had happened to Luba; she had simply stopped cleaning. Apparently she had converted to some religion – she even called me to apologise in her deep voice, tinged with a note of deranged tragedy, "for all the harm I've caused", which made me feel extremely uneasy. She had given up wearing a hat, revealing her grey roots to the world, and several times she raised a finger towards the cracks in the walls and said to Mykola: "The time is nigh!"

The stairwell was wreathed in white dust, and our shoes were covered in powder, just like that dead navvy's boots. Mykola invited students and lecturers to the house, haunted the corridors at the city council, and went for coffee with gentlemen with bad haircuts and ill-fitting suits. Thanks to him, we even had a visit from a television crew: a half-cut female reporter in silver stilettos and her highly inebriated cameraman, with a V.H.S. camcorder, smoked several fags outside the front door, and that evening a mishmash went out on the airwaves about Lviv's Sainte-Chapelle, "Ukrainian art nouveau", and the big businessman and patron who "is going to save this work of art from destruction". The identity of this saviour was yet to be revealed. We sent the first emails we had ever written to our friends in Poland: they wore well-cut clothes and modern glasses, and they knew about art. I pinned my greatest hopes on them.

I remember the day in early August when the first pieces of stained-glass cracked. Mykola gave me a technical explanation, that under pressure from the outside, the joints of the lead frames loosen, and the surfaces bend and push the glass out. I looked at the stained-glass window and saw that it was rippling. I realised that it wasn't a harmless breeze, but a lethal storm. New gaps had appeared just below the roots of the oak tree, joining up with the long-gone realm of fire – the nothingness was spreading, like in the film "The NeverEnding Story". That day, Mykola studiously filled me up, steadily rocking me to and fro as we leaned against the windowsill, with the stained-glass window just behind me. I was sure Luba was watching us through the peephole.

"I can't bear to think about it anymore."

"It's our duty to think. If not us, who? If not now, when? We are the last of the Mohicans. We're the only ones who are not indifferent to the fact that Lviv is dying. We cannot desert it, we cannot betray it."

My final conversation with Aba took place in August too. After our expedition out of town I discovered that a tick had got into my navel. A couple of days later my navel had swollen, and it felt as if the tick was expanding, while I was shrinking. I went into Aba's room, and sat down on the edge of the couch. I wanted her to make it up with me, to forgive me, to save me, as in the past. But she wasn't going to give up her righteous wrath. Angrily she poured sunflower oil into my navel. Irritably she tried to press the tick out with her fingernails. Furiously she tore its head off with a pair of tweezers. Once she had achieved her end, she lay down on the couch, and without a word turned her back on me. I went on sitting beside her, staring at the picture of General Kościuszko at the head of his peasant uprising, and spotting the imperfections in the composition. To this day I keep asking myself the question, why didn't I forcibly embrace her? Why didn't I kiss her? Why didn't I shout out everything that I was feeling?

The man who had bought the plot bordering our house drove a gold jeep, but he wasn't bald, or fat, and there were glints of shrewdness in his eyes. We caught him at the entrance to the building site. Mykola spoke, while I stood beside him, holding his hand. The fellow responded politely.

"But of course, please don't be alarmed," he said. "I'm not some *nouveau riche* boor who only cares about cash. I've heard about the stained-glass window, and I realise it's unique. I'm determined to save it. I've already got all the necessary documents from the local authorities to have it taken down, I'm just waiting for the go-ahead from Kiev, because the house is listed in the Ukrainian National Register of Historic Monuments. As soon as we get permission, the window will be renovated, and then it'll be installed in the hotel I'm building next door. It'll be permanently protected there."

Mykola squeezed my fingers painfully.

"That's utter barbarism!" he shouted. "The stained-glass window is integral to the structure of this particular building! Together they form an organic whole. Removing it from there is like tearing out your liver! Ordinary people won't have access to the hotel. First you destroy a historic building with your irresponsible construction project, and now you want to strip it of a work of art that was created for it."

The man nodded tolerantly, handed each of us a business card and drove away in his gold jeep.

This drama had one more act. Towards the end of August, Mykola was in Warsaw, and managed to reach the relevant people at the Ministry of Culture. They were persuaded by his arguments about Polish heritage, and agreed to finance the renovation of the house and the stained-glass window, which in this scenario would categorically remain in place. All that was needed was the consent of the authorities in Lviv. We tried to obtain it, but first the official responsible for such matters was on leave, and when we finally did have a meeting with her, following a specious introduction on the topic of procedures and documents she screamed that we were in the sovereign Ukrainian state, which took care of its historic buildings for itself, and that the authorities in the "Cossack city of Lviv" would never allow the citizens of another country to meddle in its internal affairs. And our doings were tantamount to betraying our homeland. Her gold shiny top tightly hugged her pear-shaped breasts and apple-shaped belly. Gazing at us from her office wall were the dopey eyes of the local Buddha, Cossack Mamay.

And then Mykola finished his surprise sculpture, which was meant to be ready by September. I had guessed what it would be from the start. After all, Lviv is not a very large city, and leaked information got around. But I only saw it with my own eyes at the unveiling ceremony.

This time, just a handful of people assembled, and there was no fanfare, no band and no choir – just the roar of the yellow minibuses moving along Svoboda Avenue. And even though at the former site of the monument with the gravestones hidden in its pedestal there were now flowerbeds with plants growing in them, I was reminded of the show I'd seen here, also in September, several years ago. This time the crowd gathered by the stage door – beside the steps which Mama used to climb on her way to work each day. The new memorial plaque was decorated with a blue-and-yellow ribbon, which was cut by the city mayor, such a small fellow that he had to use a special footstool. Next to him wobbled the stout figure of the official we'd met at the architectural department, wearing a tight, black, traditional embroidered shirt. Standing nearby, Mykola's wife was in total contrast to her: tall and stick-thin, in a light, flowing dress. She had a white band in her hair, like the ones worn by the students who went on hunger strike in 1990. There was a separate, cigarette-smoking cluster of students from the academy wearing bead bracelets, but I stood apart from them. Mykola's sculptor friend who specialised in busts of Shevchenko was also there: messy grey moustache, eyes foggy with alcohol. "Boundless cultural legacy . . . thorny path of martyrdom . . . rebuilding the new Ukraine . . . '*Bury me and then rise up, break your heavy chains*'," he thundered into a defective microphone.

The square outside the Opera roared. A column of youths in grey shirts came marching straight towards us, carrying red-and-black flags and singing something bellicose. They had metal badges on their chests with the letters "I.N.", standing for "Idea of Nation", in a shape similar to a swastika. I shuddered as it crossed my mind that they had come to protest against honouring a woman who was not an ethnic Ukrainian on the walls of the National Opera and Ballet Theatre. But the marching youths fell silent and stopped on the right-hand side of the plaque – good heavens, they had come to pay tribute to Mama.

Mykola was standing to the left, on his own. For this solemn occasion he had put on an unembroidered ash-grey shirt, to which his long hair was closer and closer in colour. He was the picture of noble indifference: the great artist whom nobody understands. He wouldn't condescend to look at anyone or anything – he stared adoringly into the distance, invisible beyond the houses.

But I was looking the whole time. At the pretty good composition of the low relief, which actually looked like a high one. But which was hung much too low down, bore no relation to its surroundings, and was a perfect match for the ghastly modern growths that infested the city's walls. Yet another Barbie-made-in-Ukraine was glaring at me from the plaque, uselessly opening her fish-like mouth to sing – through the sounds killed along with her she was meant to be rallying the crowd of flag-waving little robots to fight. I looked and looked at her. And then I too covered my eyes with an artistic veil. First, a small eighteenth-century altar appeared behind her, carved by Sebastian Fesinger with a relief sculpture of Saint Marianna – white, alabaster, dream-like; then out of the translucent surface of the stone shone skin coated in freckles and unwanted fine hairs, here and there rough to the touch like velour, in other spots smooth as satin. And there were the long fingernails, and the eyes with amber-yellow suns around the pupils. I tried to summon up the memory of the voice too, but I failed: I could hear nothing but the rattle of inefficient public transport. The plaque was cast in bronze, so in time it would turn green. Jumping ahead of events, I can say that it did indeed. And the members of the nationalist youth movement, which changed its name and uniform several times after that, took to lighting votive candles underneath it. On November 1, January 1 and in July, on the anniversary of her death.

Suddenly a new peal of thunder sounded, and I thought with relief that the ancient fears had finally come true, and the theatre building had started to sink into the ground, but it was a patriotic song to mark the end of the ceremony.

Then there was applause. The mayor shook Mykola's hand, and then, taking the footstool with him, drove away in his black Volvo to the Town Hall, just a few hundred metres away. I watched as Mykola introduced the woman from the architectural department to his wife, and as the three of them chatted. Then I slowly began to walk home.

Mykola caught me up outside the Ethnographic Museum.

"I'll be waiting at eight in front of the Boim Chapel," he whispered in my ear. He could really have said it aloud: everyone knew about us anyway. From a safe distance his wife's gauzy sleeve waved to me, and the woman herself smiled, bony and insincere.

I didn't go to the Boim Chapel – I wanted to be on my own. First I thought of going round and round on a tram, but I was too afraid of the ticket inspectors, so I walked about the city, Pohulyanka Street, Lychakiv cemetery, then the High Castle. When it grew dark, I lay in a wet meadow in Kaiserwald, where the ants and mosquitoes bit me. Meanwhile they were looking for me everywhere: in the Cathedral, at Mykola's, and also via various telephone numbers in my address book. I reached the construction site at about half past six, on a cloudless, sunny morning, as fresh as though it had unfurled above the cypresses of a Mediterranean resort, and not this city, worn out by history. I missed the ambulance by a few minutes – it had come to take Aba away, after the stroke she'd had in the night.

The Maidan

It's a cramped smell, I thought, if a smell can be defined like that; the sweetness in it was repulsive and unnecessary, bordering on decay – it brought to mind a box of half-rotten apples, maybe not so much rotten, as sour, the kind that have lain in the cellar for months on end. And for days on end I wept, not through my eyes but my nose, which poured out embarrassing fluids that I couldn't hold back; I couldn't smell anything either – not cigarettes, nor my favourite scent, but then I'd only swallowed a mouthful of gas on Hrushevsky Street, while that boy had had a stun grenade go off at his feet, destroying his eyes.

The gas that smelled of rotten apples – extremely nasty, banned by all the international conventions – got into my stomach, and I ran after it, I descended into my own inside despite the damaged pathway, and then I started weeping through my nose, pouring out of myself like a stream, like a river hidden beneath the shell of the city. I wept for the eyes of that boy: open they were the colour blue, extinguished they looked like rainbows, with yellow, green and violet rays surrounding them, more and more brightly, because he smiled all the time. He smiled as the situation at the hospital in Kiev turned dangerous and he had to be taken out of there, he smiled as he lay in an old Lada being driven away, and he even smiled once the long wait for his sight to return had begun.

My sense of smell returned when a bullet hit a paramedic's bag and the drugs spilled out; despite my ailing sinuses I smelled their sharp odour, the smell of sickness and panic. This feeling was reinforced by the wailing of sirens, the sort used to lead sailors astray, but nobody believed them, and we kept on going, up Institutska Street towards parliament, in loose ranks. So, Mama, how do you feel about the revolution happening without you? I asked inwardly. To my right, a twenty-year-old couple in big hoods were marching, wrapped in a huge blue-and-yellow flag that they were holding up on either side, as if it were a sheet that they'd spread out in a meadow at the end of the day to make love on repeatedly. To my left, I could see a stout man in camouflage, with furrows on his face like the unrepaired roads in the Ukrainian provinces, carrying a home-made wooden shield, and smoking. Ahead of me walked another man in an expensive overcoat, patent leather shoes and a hard hat speckled with traditional Easter egg motifs, holding in one hand both the red-and-white Polish flag and the red-and-black Ukrainian Nationalist flag, and it crossed my mind that red really is a popular element where flags are concerned – there's no helping it, Mama. The man had just shouted "They're shooting", and from that moment I couldn't shake off the impression that what was happening here was at odds with this city, with its ordinary streets, with the modernised grocery on the corner. Several other people shouted out the same words, but nobody turned back or started to run downhill.

There was a smell of smoke, and at the far end of the street we could see an immobile ring of black porcupines; a bonfire was burning in front of them, and there was fear of an attack – someone passed me a tyre from behind, which I was meant to roll higher, into the next pair of hands. On we went up the hill, recording ourselves and them on mobile phones and tablets, as if these devices were magic wands, thanks to which death displayed on a screen would cease to be death. There were snipers lurking on the roofs – we could hear intermittent dull cracks, while the guys in medical rescue vests darted below the balconies and carried the wounded towards the Maidan. At least they can't shoot that boy, I thought, he's safe, he's in Poland. Squares of sunlight stuck to the houses, as black and white smoke rose above them by turns, as if from the chimney of a crazed Vatican, from somewhere among the roofs full headlights were warning us, merging with the wine-red rivers that were pouring out of people's bodies and flowing down them, creating a map of freedom, the beast that has been demanding fresh blood for centuries – you were not alone, Mama. A doctor with a red cross on the singlet worn over his coat was kissing or reviving a man lying on the ground, as the wind tugged at his hair as if trying to raise his head and then the rest of him too. The streets were arching their flinty spines, making it easier for us to remove the stones from them, just like the tyres we were passing from hand to hand and throwing at the porcupines: in this war, the streets were on our side. In the cobble-throwing chain ahead of me was a lady in an outmoded felt hat, with no gloves, and her hands were bleeding, which blended in with her manicure, old age fought for us, side by side with youth. History had been forcing its way through doors and windows into our lives for ever, Mama, but here I was, walking along without a helmet, I'd ceased to defend myself against it. A boy with a rucksack, the image of that other one, jumped out in front of a row of metal shields and threw his David's stone at them, as I walked towards him, holding my mobile phone in my raised hand, recording.

Kraków, 2010–14